IT'S NOW OR NEVER

JILL STEEPLES

Boldw**oo**d

First published in 2015. This edition first published in Great Britain in 2024 by Boldwood Books Ltd.

Copyright © Jill Steeples, 2015

Cover Design by Head Design Ltd

Cover Photography: Shutterstock

The moral right of Jill Steeples to be identified as the author of this work has been asserted in accordance with the Copyright, Designs and Patents Act 1988.

Every effort has been made to obtain the necessary permissions with reference to copyright material, both illustrative and quoted. We apologise for any omissions in this respect and will be pleased to make the appropriate acknowledgements in any future edition.

A CIP catalogue record for this book is available from the British Library.

Paperback ISBN 978-1-78513-811-9

Large Print ISBN 978-1-78513-807-2

Hardback ISBN 978-1-78513-806-5

Ebook ISBN 978-1-78513-804-1

Kindle ISBN 978-1-78513-805-8

Audio CD ISBN 978-1-78513-812-6

MP3 CD ISBN 978-1-78513-809-6

Digital audio download ISBN 978-1-78513-803-4

Boldwood Books Ltd
23 Bowerdean Street
London SW6 3TN
www.boldwoodbooks.com

PROLOGUE

I suppose I was curious about that damned letter. Who wouldn't be? It was addressed to me, after all, and it was meant to hold all the secrets to my dazzling future. In that situation I'd defy anyone not to want to know what was held within that envelope. Part of me saw it as an elaborate joke and I wondered if that was what the funny gorgeous stranger had intended, but there was also a small part of me that couldn't help thinking that he might know something I didn't. Wouldn't that be cool? To think my whole life was known to someone else but not to me?

The thing was, I'd managed to catch a few tantalising snippets which had only stirred my interest more, but as I'd craned my head to read further, the 'all-knowing one' had pulled an arm around the sheet of paper as he wrote, blocking my view to what he was furiously scribbling down.

You think that's mad?
pretty momentous
mind-blowing to say the least.
secrets... hidden
Forever.

...not only me involved
stalkerish
at my side
tomorrow...

Stalkerish? What the hell! And tomorrow? Well today was tomorrow, if you get my drift, and that letter had my name written all over it – so where was the problem?

In the late morning chill of an April morning, the wine bar looked far less salubrious than it had the previous evening. There was an air of neglect and disappointment about the place as though it was carefully nurturing its own hangover, a bit like me, but I wasn't worried about that. There was only one thing on my mind and that was getting my hands on that letter.

Through the tinted windows, my hands held up to the glass, I saw a young woman in black trousers, black top and white apron behind the bar, wiping down tops and polishing glasses. I took the opportunity, pushing through the door with my shoulder.

'Sorry, we're not actually open yet.' The woman turned, glancing at her watch. 'If you could come back in half an hour we should be ready for you.'

She probably thought I had a drink problem, it was only ten thirty in the morning.

'Oh no, I don't want a drink. It's just that I was in here last night and I left something behind.'

'Ah okay. What was it? I'll take a look for you.'

'It was an envelope with my name on it. Jen Faraday. The guy I was with left it behind the bar for me.'

Her eyebrows flickered at me doubtfully before she wandered off, straight to the till, where she retrieved the envelope from the small gap down the side and waved it in the air.

'This is it, isn't it,' she said, still holding it aloft.

'Yes, thank you.'

I held out my hand to take it from her, but she snatched it away, a triumphant smile on her face.

'I'm really sorry, but I can't give it to you. It says quite clearly on here, "not to be opened until April of next year". That's a whole year away. Sorry,' she said, far too delightedly for her own good.

'Yes, but it is actually my envelope, for me,' I said, getting irritated now by her unwavering presence between me and the letter. 'Could I just have it please?'

'No.'

'Right.' I leant over and snatched it out of her hands – quick as a ninja warrior, she snatched it right back again. For a moment there I thought about tackling her, grappling her to the floor, and reclaiming what was rightfully mine, but I was worried about being arrested and ending up in a prison cell for common assault. Besides, weighing up the situation, she seemed much more agile and fitter than me and I had a suspicion I would be the one to come off worse in any wrestling competition.

'Right,' I said again, with authority this time. 'Just to let you know, I will be speaking to your manager about this.'

'I am the manager.'

'Right. Well, that's fine. Absolutely fine.'

I turned on my tail and marched out of that wine bar, determined never to set foot in there again. Well, not for another year at least. That's if I hadn't forgotten all about that wretched letter by then.

1

'You're what?'

'I know! It's all a bit mad. It's been a bit of a whirlwind actually. Everything's happened so quickly, but I wanted you to be the first to know.'

Woah! Hang on a minute here. This couldn't be so. Some things in life are taken as a given and right at the top of the list of given things was, *numero uno*:

I, Jen Faraday, would be the first to marry out of me and my best friend, Angie, because I am the marrying type. And Angie is not. And I'd been in a nine-year relationship with my long-term boyfriend, Paul, who was the reliable steady type, and with whom I'd visited bridal fairs and drawn up invitation lists and decided on a colour scheme. Coral and mint, in case you're interested. Angie wasn't even in a relationship because she'd ditched her on-off totally unreliable scumbag of a boyfriend because of his wayward tendencies.

Admittedly, there had been a slight hitch to my plans when my reliable steady boyfriend had shown a bit of uncharacteristic get-up-and-go and had... got up and gone, deciding that he didn't want to get married after all. Well, not to me, at least. Paul convinced me it was a mutual decision, that it was the right thing for us both, but on reflection I think it was more mutual on his part than on my own. Within three months he'd met someone new, married her and now they were expecting their first baby together. Who doesn't love a happy ending?

'It's Tom actually. We're back together.' Angie did have the good grace to look sheepish as she imparted this bit of earth-shattering news. 'We're going to make a go of it.'

'Tom? Scumbag, grotbag Tom? But you said...'

'I know what I said, but he's changed, honestly, he has. And please don't call him that, Jen. Not any more. The break up was the best thing that could ever have happened to us. It's made us realise how we feel about each other. We want to spend the rest of our lives together.'

'Blimey.'

A tiny part of me died inside. No, scrub that. A huge part of me died. Angie was my partner in crime, my soul sister on the singles dating scene. How would I ever cope in those murky waters without her?

'Are you sure you know what you're doing?' I protested, trying to push my feelings to one side. 'I'd hate to think you were making a mistake. You were doing so well, Angie, getting over Tom. Why go back? Isn't that what you're always telling me? That I need to look forward and not dwell on the past?'

'That's the whole point, Jen. I'm not going backwards. I'm moving forward with Tom. A new promise, a new life together. I know this must be difficult for you, after everything that happened with Paul, but I hoped you'd be happy for me. Tom and I are very much in love.'

Eugh! I resisted the urge to throw up over the carpet. The

only thing stopping me was the fact that it was my carpet and I'd be the one to have to clean up the mess.

Love? Ha! I thought I knew what love was until Paul had pulled the rug from beneath my feet. And if I could get it quite so wrong after nine years, how would I ever be able to know how to get it right again? Against all the odds Angie had managed it and now, without so much as a backwards glance, she was leaving me behind, floundering all alone in a lonely single wilderness. Every part of my life had hit the buffers. I'd come to a shuddering halt with a neon 'No Way Out' sign flashing in front of me, while everyone around me was moving forward with their lives, going off in exciting new directions.

Panic constricted my throat.

'Wait for me,' I wanted to shout. The life train was about to leave the station and I hadn't even bought my ticket yet.

I consumed a sigh, remembering this wasn't about me and I should at least pretend to be happy for Angie.

'Look, if this is really what you want, then of course I'm happy for you,' I said, not entirely convincingly.

To be honest, it wasn't only Angie's unexpected imminent departure over to the other side that was depressing me. For months now I'd been fighting the feeling that I'd stepped into a gooey patch of quagmire on the way to my full and exciting life and somehow I'd got stuck, knee high in a puddle that I had little hope of pulling my feet out of.

My love life was non-existent, I'd been stuck in the same job for years and I'd suddenly realised that all those things I was going to do when I was a fresh-faced eighteen-year-old straight out of school just hadn't happened. I hadn't gone to university, I hadn't travelled the world, I hadn't had a mad and passionate affair with a suave older man and I hadn't even been sky-diving or skinny-dipping in an azure-blue sea. The list of things I hadn't done yet was endless.

It didn't help that Gramps was acting like a lovestruck teenager too. When your elderly granddad was seeing more action than you were then something was definitely wrong. Honestly, it was ridiculous. Only the other day I'd popped round to see him and found him up in the spare bedroom, surrounded by cardboard boxes and black bags.

'What are you doing?'

'I only came up here to find my best shirt. The one with the double cuffs. I'm off to a tea dance this afternoon with the lovely Marcia.' He adopted a dancing hold and gave a twirl around the spare bedroom, a bloom to his cheeks. 'But then I got distracted by all this mess. I think this room is well overdue a clear out, don't you? Maybe I'll give it a fresh lick of paint too.'

I grunted my reply. Marcia was bossy and brash, wore over-bright orange lipstick and heels I suspected were far too high for a woman of her age. I didn't know what Gramps saw in her.

I cast a gaze over the room with its daisy sprig wallpaper and soft yellow curtains. I'd slept in this room hundreds of times over the years, as a child and then as a teenager, and even now occasionally at Christmas and Easter – the room's cosy familiarity was always fondly reassuring. Why mess with things now?

'Aren't those Nan's old knitting magazines?' I said, noticing the pile by the doorway.

'Yes, they're no good here just gathering dust, are they? And unless you have any plans to take up knitting in the near future I can't see any reason to keep them.'

'Oh...' I looked at Gramps, his shirt hanging expectantly on the door frame with its promise of tango nights full of love and passion, and I felt a pang of sadness for my nan. What would she have to say? She wouldn't be happy about those magazines. Or Marcia. To be sure.

'It's up to you,' I said, forcing a smile. 'Throw them away if you want to.'

'What I did find though,' he said, looking at me with a pensive smile on his lips, 'was this.' He picked up a book of poetry from the bookcase in the corner and pulled out a piece of paper. 'It's a copy of that letter from your mum. You know, the one she left for you in with her personal bits and pieces.'

'Really? I didn't realise you had a copy too. Mine's at home. In a shoebox on the top of the wardrobe.'

I'd read it once on the day of her funeral, over eight years ago now, and then consigned it to its current resting place. Funny, I found it hard to recall what was in that letter now.

'I think she wanted me to have a copy just in case you lost yours or decided to throw it away. Do you want it?' he asked, holding the folded up piece of paper towards me. I took it from his hands and opened it up, the vivid reminder of my mum's distinctive handwriting pulling at my heartstrings.

I plopped down on the single bed and paused for a moment or two, turning the letter over in my hands. I took a deep breath and began to read.

My dearest darling Jennifer,

This is undoubtedly the hardest letter I will ever have to write, but I wanted to leave you with something, just a brief note, that might bring you some comfort in the coming months and years. Hopefully, when you come to read it you will hear my voice as if I'm standing in the same room as you because I honestly believe I will never be that far away. Funny really because now I've picked up the pen I'm not sure what it is I want to say, only that you mustn't feel sad or scared because now I've come to terms with what is happening, what is my fate, I'm feeling neither of those things.

What I must say is that you are the most amazing, beautiful and special daughter and I feel so lucky and privileged to have had you in my life. You are very much loved by me and, of course, Nan and Gramps, and you can never know how much joy and pleasure you've brought and will continue to bring to our family.

I'm sad, of course, that I won't be around to see you blossom into the amazing young woman you are destined to be. I mean, you already are that woman, but I know there's so much more to come from you and you have a dazzling future ahead of you.

What possible advice can I have to give you? Only to be brave and to live your life to the full and take all the opportunities you are given. It's true, life is short, so we need to make the most of every minute we have here. I know I've passed my 'worry' gene on to you and I apologise for that! Possibly that's one of my only regrets, spending too much time worrying about things that never happened. I wish I'd been braver, bolder, taken more chances, laughed more, loved more, got drunk more, eaten that extra slice of pizza and had the big wedge of chocolate brownie for pudding instead of being 'good' and I so wish I hadn't worried so much about what other people thought about me. It really doesn't matter! If you can, lovely Jen, send that pesky 'worry' gene packing and grab hold of your life by the scruff of its neck.

You still have the time Jen, to do all those things you want to do. Basically, all I would say is get out there and enjoy yourself. Don't sweat the small stuff, and the big stuff, well, I have a sneaky suspicion that looks after itself anyway.

I have a feeling that in ten years from now you'll be in a great place. I can only imagine what terrific things the future holds for you: a fulfilling career, a home by the sea or perhaps a city apartment, a gorgeous husband (or not – I couldn't really recommend marriage, but I know lots of people speak very highly of the institution), six beautiful children (I can definitely recommend having children – I only wish I'd had more so you'd have some siblings to share your future with), a golden labrador (ah, that could be my other regret, never getting the dog). Anyway, who knows? It might be none of those things; you might want to take a vow of silence and commit your life to God. Whatever it is, I don't care, darling. I just want you to be happy in whatever it is you choose to do. If you can promise me one thing, it would be that!

I love you very much sweetheart, today, tomorrow and always, and you'll always be here in my heart.

Keep an eye out for your Nan and Gramps, as they will for you, I know.

Love, Mum xxx

P.S. Chuck out those scales! Now, do it now! Don't waste another moment worrying about how much you weigh. Another half a stone or two isn't going to kill you. You're beautiful as you are. Remember that. Chin up, head held high and embrace your inner gorgeousness. Lord knows, you've got plenty to call on. Lots of love, darling. Mum xxx

I tipped my head back to look at the ceiling, the memories rushing back. Gramps placed a hand on my shoulder and I could feel the tears brimming in my eyes. Mum was right. I could hear her voice clearly, as if she'd just made an unscheduled visit from high up above and had wafted down into the spare bedroom. I could see her big wide smile, the way her bright blue eyes lit up her face and could feel her breath against my cheek, the warm, caressive tones to her voice echoing around the little room.

What would I say to her if she was here now?

'Oh hi, Mum! That letter you wrote to me, the one about being brave and bold, and living life to the full. Yep, really good advice, only I haven't actually done anything about it yet. I was just going to get round to it soon.'

Would she still think I was an amazing young woman or would she feel disappointed that I hadn't taken my chances? I blinked away a rogue tear that threatened to fall and folded up the letter again in my lap.

'You all right, love?'

'Yeah, I'm fine! It's just... reading the letter again, it makes me realise...' My words trailed away as I looked up at Gramps and smiled, my gaze travelling around the little room. I batted away the pang of nostalgia stirring in my stomach. Like me, this room was stuck in a time warp. We were both in desperate need of an overhaul.

A sense of urgency consumed me. I wanted to be that woman Mum was so certain I was destined to be. What the hell was I waiting for?

'Come on, Jen,' I could hear Mum whispering in my ear, *'It's now or never!'*

2

A couple of days later at work, I summoned up what little courage I had, took a deep breath and approached my boss.

'Can I have a minute please, Matt?'

'Yeah sure, go through to the office. I'll grab us a coffee.'

In fairness, I had actually tried to hand in my notice to Matt on three separate occasions already this year. My resignation letter had been growing worn and tatty in my pocket for some time now, but each time I tried to do the deed my attempts were thwarted by one thing or another.

So it shouldn't have been any surprise to me that it was a full twenty minutes later before Matt backed his way through the door, juggling two mugs of coffee in his hands. Matt was a very hands-on boss. If there was a problem then he would be there sorting it out. He much preferred to be outside, more often than not zooming up and down the yard on a fork-lift truck, but he was just as happy to be on the shop floor lending a hand at the tills and chatting away cheerily to the customers.

'Sorry about that, I got waylaid!' He had a big apologetic smile on his face. He shoved a couple of cardboard boxes away with his foot and with difficulty found a rare empty spot on his messy desk to place the brimming mugs, sending a whole heap of paperwork scattering to the floor in the process. I smiled and leant down to collect the papers, returning them to his desk.

'Oh, don't worry about that. I'll pick them up later.' He sat down in his leather swivel chair and gave a little side-to-side jiggle. 'So what was it you wanted to speak to me about then?'

'Well...'

I wondered if I wasn't about to make the biggest mistake of my life. Matt was much more than a boss to me. Over the years he'd been a mentor, a funny and supportive colleague, and always a friend.

Today he was wearing the Browns standard issue green polo shirt, the same one that all the employees wore, with brown khaki waterproof trousers and big black boots. It only occurred to me now that with his tall, broad build and his well-defined physique, out of all the workforce, Matt probably suited the company uniform best of all. To be honest, with my mid-brown hair (mousy to anyone being unkind) and pale skin (pasty, to the unkind lady over there) it had never really done me any favours.

In comparison, it did Matt many favours. I wondered for the first time if he hadn't chosen the earthy colours of the corporate identity to complement the warm brown of his eyes and the chestnut hue of his unruly curly hair. His strong, defined fore-arms were a deep golden brown, testament to the number of hours he spent outdoors, where he could always be found lending a hand to any department where there might be a short-fall of labour that day. You rarely saw Matt suited and booted or sitting behind his desk, come to that. Which probably explained the mess...

'The thing is, Matt...' I faltered. Why was I suddenly distracted by the colour of his eyes? It wasn't too late to change my mind, to come up with an excuse for why I needed to talk to him.

'The thing is, Matt. I wanted to give you this.' Boldly, I handed over the envelope with my letter of resignation inside. Too late for backing out now.

He looked askance, at me and then at the envelope.

'What is it?'

'I'm really sorry, but I've decided it's time for me to move on. It's my resignation,' I added, in case he was in any doubt.

He fell silent, pulled the letter out, furrowed his brow as his eyes scanned the words, before he looked across at me again. His expression was filled with disappointment.

'What? Why? You can't leave! I won't allow it. You're my right-hand man, Jen. A central player in the Browns team. Why would you want to leave?'

I squirmed in my seat, my hands clasped together tightly in my lap. That was a good question. It would have been so much easier if I could have told him that I had a brilliant new job to go to, or that I was going off to university to study something unfathomable or I was rushing off to marry my soulmate and we were going to sail around the world together, but I had no such excuses.

'Well, you know when I joined Browns it was only ever intended to be a temporary summer job, and that was nine years ago.'

'Yes, and look at you now, Jen! You're part of the Browns family. How will we ever manage without you?'

'You will,' I said, with a small smile. 'Look, I just wanted to let you know my plans, although I'm in no desperate hurry to get away so can give you a few months' notice. I don't want to leave you in the lurch for the busy summer season.'

'Right, I see...' Matt's disappointment was so palpable that I almost felt like saying *'no, don't worry, I didn't mean it,'* but I was determined to hold on to my resolve this time.

It had been my first job after finishing my A-levels, a way to earn some extra cash before going off to university in the September, but when Mum fell ill everything changed. There was no way I was going to leave her and move three hundred miles to the other end of country. A gap year spent working at the garden centre and nursing Mum back to health would have been the perfect compromise, but it wasn't as straightforward as that. Mum's illness was long and drawn out and when she died two years' later, my desire to go to uni died with her. In the long and dark days following her death, my job had been a lifeline; it gave me something to wake up for in the mornings, a comforting routine that brought an element of normality to my life. Matt had been instrumental in offering me that small sense of hope.

Since then I'd worked in every department there was; from serving in the restaurant, to working outside caring for the plants, to sourcing items for the gift store, which had become my permanent role over the last couple of years.

Being part of the Browns family felt safe and reassuring, but sometimes those family ties could be suffocating.

'If I don't leave now, I might never leave. I might spend the rest of my life here, picking up my pension when I'm a very old lady.'

Matt grunted.

'And would that be such a bad thing?'

I laughed. Obviously it wouldn't seem that way to Matt. This was his life. He'd been brought up in the business, it was all he'd ever known. The success of the store today was down hugely to Matt's hard work and commitment and he could be proud of that, but to me it was ultimately just a job.

'I'm sorry, Matt. I promise you it's nothing personal. It's just something I feel I need to do right now.'

'Well, I can't say I'm not saddened by this news. Is there nothing I can do to make you change your mind? If it's about the money then I'm sure we could come to some arrangement.'

'No, it's not about the money or even the job. I've loved working here, you know that, and I've made so many good friends. It's just the right time for me to move on.'

'Well, I can't say that I'm not disappointed. What will you do?'

'I've got lots of plans, although none of them are fully formed yet,' I said with a grimace. 'I'll take on some part-time work so that I can still pay the bills, but I'd like to write more articles for the gardening magazines. I've had a little bit of success there, but I'd like to devote more time to my writing and growing my online presence so that I can pass on my own gardening hints and ideas to a wider audience. Young single people or elderly people living alone, newly married couples, people who don't have much outdoor space, but who still want to find a way to bring some greenery, a touch of the outdoors, into their lives.'

'Sounds very inspiring.'

'I've also been thinking about developing a range of savoury jams and chutneys. Similar to those we're already selling in the food store, but maybe experimenting with some different variations.'

'Really? I didn't know you were a cook.'

'I'm not. But I love pickles and chutneys, or anything in a pretty jar come to that, so I thought I could learn how to make them. How difficult can it be?'

Matt raised his eyebrows and smiled at me, as though he thought I might be mad. The same thought had actually occurred to me.

'I'll probably have to sign up to a temp agency to see me over for a few months while I settle on what to do, but I think it will be good for me. You have to remember, I've only ever worked here. I don't know what it's like to work for another company.'

'Not as good as working for Browns, that's for sure,' said Matt, a rueful smile on his lips.

I wondered if that might be true; that I might never find such a friendly and interesting company to work for, but it was too late for those kind of worries now. I'd done it! After all the prevaricating, I'd finally handed my notice in and taken the first small step on my way to a brand new exciting chapter in my life.

3

Ms Angela Peters
and
Mr Tom Sidney Cooper
request the pleasure of your company
at their marriage
on Saturday 19th April
at 1.30 p.m.
at Casterton Registry Office, Bucks
followed by lunch at Chez Michel

'Jen, over here!'

I walked up the stone steps of the town hall – one arm held against my forehead blocking out the warm rays of the sun – just managing to make out the small huddle of people congregating outside the doors.

'Look at you,' I said, my gaze alighting on Angie when I reached the top of the steps. She was wearing a simple cream linen shift dress with a scalloped collar and hemline, and a matching pashmina wrapped around her shoulders. Her strawberry blonde hair was tied in a French plaint at the back of her head. 'You look absolutely stunning,' I whispered in her ear as she grabbed me for a hug. Beautiful, radiant and utterly feminine too. Almost unrecognisable from the Angie I knew and loved, who spent most of her time in cargo trousers, crop tops and Doc Martens.

'Hi Tom, lovely to see you!' I said, turning to the groom, trying to sound as though I meant it while the words 'scumbag, grotbag' played over in my head. 'Congratulations!'

'Thanks, Jen. Yeah, who'd have thought it, eh? It's been a while.'

Maybe I imagined the awkwardness as he leant in to give me a chaste kiss on the cheek or perhaps it was just because I hadn't seen him since they'd got back together again. He looked much more handsome in his sleek grey suit than I remembered him to be. Clutching Angie's hand, looking fondly into her eyes, he looked every inch the devoted husband-to-be. Perhaps he really had changed after all, and if Angie had found it in her heart to forgive Tom, then maybe I should do the same too.

Be gone with you, scumbag, grotbag and all the other uncharitable names I had for Tom. I allowed my remaining reservations about him and this whirlwind marriage to flutter off in the light spring breeze. This was their special day and, as Angie's best friend, I was determined to celebrate it with them.

Putting all negative thoughts out of my head I wandered off and said my hellos to some of the other guests and chatted briefly with Angie's mum and dad, before Angie grabbed me by the arm and led me away.

'Let me introduce you to Alex. I don't think you two have met before, have you? Alex and Tom used to work in the city together. Alex, this is my very best friend in the whole wide world, Jen.'

She'd brought me to a standstill in front of the man who was clearly auditioning for the part of most gorgeous wedding guest. In my opinion, without even seeing all the other guests, he'd won the part hands down. I looked up at him and smiled.

'Delighted to meet you, Jen,' he said, lifting up my hand and depositing the lightest of kisses on my fingertips in a gesture so gallant and ridiculously over-the-top it made my toes curl.

There's something about a man in a navy blue suit and a crisp double cuffed white shirt that does funny things to my insides. Don't ask me why, but it's always been that way. Added to that the fact that this particular man was over six foot tall with dark hair and warm sparkling eyes and it made for an intriguing combination. As his lips met my fingers I caught the faintest smell of sun-drenched orange groves and I tried to ignore the flip of anticipation that turned in my stomach.

'I understand you'll be my partner in crime today?'

'Excuse me?' I hadn't been listening to his words, I'd been too busy taking a surreptitious inhalation trying to recapture the essence of that delicious scent.

'You're the other witness, right? Is it your first time too?'

'Oh yes, my first time,' I said, concentrating now on his lips, which on close inspection were full and wide and really rather lovely.

Angie had left us alone, giving my hand a gentle squeeze as she went off to greet a couple of new arrivals and I noticed those lips were now twisting in amusement.

'And do you have the slightest idea what we have to do?'

'Absolutely no idea whatsoever.'

'Brilliant, let's go and do it together then,' he said, grabbing my hand and leading me inside.

Smiling, I wandered with him into the registry office and we stood to the side of the bride and groom, who seemed oblivious to anything but each other. Tom tidied Angie's hair away from her face and whispered something into her ear which made her laugh, happiness radiating from every inch of her being.

Looking around the oak-panelled room, waiting for the registrar to start the proceedings, my eyes landed on the ring of flowers on the desk, and my breath caught at the back of my throat at the enormity of the situation. My best friend, the girl at school who was once named the least likely to get married, was doing exactly that (before me even, which was still a bit of a sore point) and things would never be the same again. It was the end of an era and the start of a brand new one and there was still a tiny part of me that felt hugely unsettled by that fact.

I clasped my hands in front of me letting the words of the registrar, a kindly middle-aged woman, wash over me. The legal formalities were all wrapped up within a matter of minutes. Tom and Angie signed the register, before Alex and I were invited to do the same, adding our names in black ink at the bottom of the page. Signed, sealed, delivered. As easily as that.

* * *

After some photos, taken by Tom's brother on the steps of the town hall and on the bridge overlooking the river, our small party took the short walk to the restaurant where we were greeted by Michel, the owner of the establishment, with welcoming glasses of champagne.

'Can you believe it?' Angie, already drunk on happiness, radiance and excitement, steered me into a quiet nook of the room. 'I'm a married woman at last. Who'd have thought it?' She waved her wedding band in front of my nose.

'Congratulations, darling. I am so happy for you. And no, I still can't quite believe it!' I lifted up her hand to examine her finger just to make sure. 'It's beautiful! Really, I hope you and

Tom have a long and happy married life together filled with love and laughter.'

Angie hugged me so tightly I thought I might faint. 'We will, Jen. We will. Just you wait and see.' She released me from her bear hold and slipped an arm around my waist.

'You do realise that this changes nothing between us. Obviously I'll now have to be made an honorary member of the Single Girls' Club but I still intend to attend our meetings in an advisory capacity only, you understand.'

'I should hope so too.'

'Definitely, our Tuesday nights are going to remain a permanent fixture on my calendar, don't you worry. I'm going to be coming round to yours and scanning those dating websites with you and I'm not going to stop until we find your Mr Right. Of course, being a married woman, I'm an expert in these matters now and so will expect to find you the perfect man in next to no time.'

'You reckon, do you?'

'Absolutely. There's no question of doubt in my mind.'

We laughed, but I knew it was never going to happen. Giggling at dating profiles had been a blast when we'd both been in the same position, single girls looking for love, but doing it on my own with Angie acting as my chaperone smacked of desperation. And I wasn't desperate. Absolutely not. Besides, I was quite capable of finding my own romantic hero if I wanted one. I certainly didn't need anyone's help on that front.

'So what do you think of Alex then?' she whispered in my ear.

I span around just to make sure he wasn't in the vicinity and his eyes locked on to mine from across the other side of the room, where he was chatting with Tom, as if he knew we were talking about him. He raised his glass of champagne in the air and hooked me with a smile.

'Well, he seems lovely. Charming and, well, just delightful really.' I don't know if it was the effects of the champagne which was being topped up to the brim of my glass faster than I could drink the stuff or whether it was the emotion of the occasion, but I was already feeling lightheaded and we hadn't even sat down to eat yet.

'Ha ha, listen to you, acting all coy and *"oh yes, he's delightful."* I've seen the way you look at him. You fancy the pants off him, don't you?'

'He's very attractive, I admit, but I'm just appreciating the beauty of a man who is clearly a fine specimen of his breed.'

'Is that right?' Angie's mouth quirked in disbelief. 'In all seriousness though, he is lovely. Totally charming, but let me just give you a word of warning. If you thought Tom was a player, and really he's not, then Alex is in another league all together. He's a love 'em and leave 'em type of guy and I think he's left plenty behind in his past. I've lost count of the number of girlfriends he's had since I've known Tom and none of them have lasted past the three month stage. If you want to keep your heart intact, then honestly, Jen, don't even go there.'

Okay, so it seemed that the lovely Alex was a scumbag/grotbag out of the same mould as his friend, Tom. It didn't surprise me in the slightest, but then I was a woman of the world and I could certainly handle the likes of Alex whatever-his-name-was. It would need more than a few appreciative glances and a couple of glasses of champagne to get past my exacting standards, I can tell you.

'That's very interesting to have the lowdown on Alex's love life, thank you, but you have absolutely no need to worry on that score. He is so not my type. All that smooth polished sophistication leaves me totally cold. Besides, I could never go out with a guy who is so much better looking than me.'

We giggled and for a moment it was as if we were back at my flat together sharing our dating woes. She took my face in her hands and kissed me on the lips.

'Listen, I ought to go and mingle, but I just want to say thank you for everything you've done for me. You've been a complete star!'

'What have I done? I haven't done anything.'

'Oh, but you have, Jen. You've done everything. You're the best friend I could ever ask for. You've always been there for me and are totally supportive and you've never told me I'm doing the wrong thing in marrying Tom. A couple of people have, you know. Oh, and back there, you were absolutely the perfect witness to my marriage. I mean you watched and witnessed the whole thing with... with aplomb.'

I burst out laughing.

'Well, it was a very difficult job, I have to tell you.'

'Honestly, I mean it. It wouldn't have been the same without you.'

I could see tears of happiness and joy brimming in her eyes.

'Go on,' I said, shooing her away before we both collapsed in an emotional heap. 'Go and see to your guests. Oh, and thank you for the warning,' I said, looking over in Alex's direction. 'I'll be sure to steer well clear.'

4

It might have been easy to heed Angie's advice if it hadn't been such a small and intimate wedding, but there were only about eighteen of us in total and as luck would have it Alex and I were placed next to each other at the lunch table.

Still there were worse problems to have than having to be wedged up against a good-looking, sweet smelling man at a wedding reception and to be honest I was quite enjoying Alex's attentiveness. He pulled out my chair, filled my water glass, flapped my napkin with a flourish in the air before laying it on my lap and generally went out of his way to make me feel completely at ease. I wasn't quite sure why Angie had gone to such lengths to warn me off him – after all, it wasn't as if I'd be likely to see him again after today.

'So,' he said, leaning into my side, his breath warm against my cheek, taunting me with his citrus loveliness again, 'how long do you give them?'

'Sorry?' I said, uncertain I'd heard him correctly.

'Angie and Tom,' he whispered. 'How long do you think it will last?'

I looked over my shoulder to see if Tom's Nana Gladys who was sitting on the other side of me had heard Alex's impertinent question but she was deep in conversation with her sister. Thank goodness! I turned back to Alex who looked as though he was actually waiting for some kind of sensible answer.

'I honestly can't believe you said that! That's a terrible question to ask. The ink's barely dry on their marriage certificate and already you're questioning how long they'll be together. That's so disrespectful. Can't you just let them have their special day and be happy for them?'

'Oh, I am happy for them. Really I am. But I know Tom of old and well...' He shrugged. 'He's never seemed like the settling down type to me. Obviously I hope it works out for them, but, you know, you can't help wondering these things, can you?'

'I haven't even given it a thought,' I said, taking a restorative sip of water from my glass. Well, actually I had given it more than a second thought, but I would never admit that to anyone else, especially someone I'd only just met. I quickly reassessed my opinion of Alex.

'Maybe it's just me then.' His mouth twisted in a way that might have been charming if I wasn't quite so irritated with him.

'Yes, I think it might be. I mean why would you even say something like that on a day like today?'

'Well, you have to admit it's a bit of a lottery, getting married.'

In profile, Alex's strong jawline and defined cheekbones lent him an air of superiority that might have been intimidating if it wasn't for the amused knowing smile that seemed to hover permanently at his lips. His eyes flickered with amusement too, particularly when he focused his gaze on me, and I wasn't sure if he was genuinely worried about the newlyweds' future or if he was being deliberately provocative. Maybe he knew something I didn't. After all, he was Tom's best friend. Mind you, Angie didn't speak very highly of Alex so perhaps he was judging Tom by his own standards.

'Hmm, well in that case we have to hope that Tom and Angie have picked out the winning ticket.'

At the other end of the table Angie's father stood up and proposed a toast to the bride and groom.

'To Tom and Angie!' We all stood up and raised our glasses to the happy couple. Angie and I exchanged a look, one that said '*I love you, best friend*', and I hoped with every fibre of my being that she really had found her happy ending. Then I chinked glasses with Alex, my gaze lingering on his face a moment too long, distracted by the colour of his eyes which earlier I could have sworn were a dark blue, but now looked to be a greeny-grey hue.

'Sure, but you have to be realistic about these things,' he said, once we were sat down again. 'You only need to look at the divorce figures to know that a lot of marriages will be doomed to failure.'

'Honestly, what are you like?'

Alex only seemed amused by my question. Distracting eyes or not, he was spoiling my mood. This was a celebration for heaven's sake. I'd put my concerns away for the day. Why couldn't he? The champagne was flowing nicely and the waiting staff had just delivered the most delicious looking slice of smoked salmon and prawn terrine to my place which was making my mouth water. I couldn't wait to tuck in.

'You are clearly not a romantic, Alex, I can tell,' I said, hoping that would put an end to that particular line of conversation. I picked up my knife and fork and looked around me to see if it was okay to start. Nothing was going to spoil my appetite today.

He laughed, a warm slow chuckle that caused me to pause, fork in air, for a moment; I hated to admit it but the sound was so intoxicating it warmed my insides.

'Quite the opposite. I am a complete romantic. That's why I would only get married if I knew for certain that I'd want to spend the rest of my life with that person.'

'What?' I gave him my best, most withering look. 'Doesn't everyone think like that when they are about to get married?' This man was talking complete and utter rubbish. 'I can't believe anyone goes into a marriage thinking it's not going to work.'

'Perhaps you're right,' he said, giving me a sideways glance and the benefit of that lazy smile again. I was wondering now if his eyes were more a hazelly brown colour. 'Still doesn't explain why so many marriages fail though.'

'Who knows, but we shouldn't be talking about such things today.' I reprimanded him lightly with a tap on his arm and he looked down at his suit where I'd touched him, as if I'd actually hurt him, and he raised an eyebrow at me with an amused expression on his face.

'Okay, well let me tell you about my gran and granddad,' Alex said, his voice warm and low so that I had to move my head closer to properly hear him. 'They met when she was sixteen and he was seventeen. Her father, who was very strict and a bit of a bully from what I've heard, tried to stop her from seeing him, so do you know what they did?'

I shook my head.

'They ran away to Gretna Green and got married. They'd only known each other for three weeks. Now is that romantic enough for you?'

'Oh gosh, that is romantic,' I said with a heartfelt sigh. 'Can you imagine? And did they have a long and happy marriage?'

'They've just celebrated their diamond wedding anniversary. We had a big party for them the other week.'

'That's so lovely,' I said, and for a moment I felt a pang of regret for my nan, who wasn't around any more to enjoy those type of celebrations with Gramps. They'd missed out on their golden anniversary by about fourteen months, but Gramps and I had been adamant that we were still going to celebrate the occasion anyway by going to Nan's favourite restaurant, eating her favourite food and toasting her memory. It had been a special but poignant day. 'Fancy only knowing someone for three weeks and then marrying them and it lasting for all those years.'

'Exactly. That's what I mean about it being a bit of a lottery. I mean you hear stories like that, but then there are those people who've lived together for years, finally decide to get married and then, within a matter of months, it's all over. I've never quite understood that either.'

Maybe Alex had a point after all.

The serving staff cleared our plates before delivering the main course, which looked like a feast. I closed my eyes and inhaled. The most delicious aromas wafted towards my nostrils; roasted duck breast, potato rosti, honey-roasted carrots and savoy cabbage.

'That actually happened to me,' I said airily, not entirely sure why I was choosing to divulge this information to a stranger.

'What?' He turned to look at me, doing a double-take. 'You're married?'

'No, I was. Well, no, I wasn't actually,' I said, not really knowing what I meant. 'I very nearly got married. Could you pass me the water please?' More water, less champagne was clearly what was required here. 'I was with someone for nine years and we were about to get married and then, well, we split up.'

'Oh, that's tough. Sorry for that.' His gaze travelled over my face, which was most unnerving when I was baring my soul. 'Nine years is like a marriage.'

'Yeah, it was just one of those things,' I said, waving my hand in front of my face in a suitably nonchalant manner as though it hadn't mattered in the slightest. 'It obviously wasn't meant to be. Maybe for those couples who have been together for a long time, getting married is a sticking plaster to cover the cracks already in the relationship, and it's only when they've made that firm commitment that they realise that they can't make it better after all.'

Alex pondered on that for a moment before tilting his head to one side and nodding his head sagely.

'That's very profound. You might have a point there.'

And I wondered as I said it if that's what had happened to Paul and me. It had been a now or never situation. We'd been together so long we either had to make a commitment or go our separate ways. It was only when we started thinking about our future, making definite plans, that we realised our future didn't belong together after all. Or else Paul realised. He was the one who instigated the end of our relationship. Maybe Alex was right. Perhaps it was more of a lottery than I thought.

'So you're suggesting, to be in with a chance of having a long and happy marriage, it's better to marry someone relatively quickly after meeting them?' He quirked his eyebrow in a way that spiked an instant response from the deepest depths of my stomach.

'Oh, I don't know about that,' I said, looking away, feeling a heat rise in my cheeks. 'I'm hardly an expert on these matters.'

I wasn't sure how we'd got on to this subject.

'You and Tom work together?' I said, desperate now to change tack.

'We used to. We were at uni together and when we left we both went to work for the same bank in the city. It was a mad time. We worked too hard, played too hard, and probably did most things to excess.' He laughed and I conjured up a mental image of them both; partying, living life to the full, two young men at the top of their game. 'Three years in that job was more than enough for me. When I'd made enough money I quit. Tom's still there though, he rode the storm out.'

'Oh right. So what is it you do now then?'

'I've an art gallery in town. The Woodland Studios? I represent a few artists locally and nationally, and sell online too. I paint a bit myself too when I get the time, which I have to admit isn't that often these days.'

'So quite a change from what you were doing before then?'

'Yep. Completely different. Now I'm doing something I really love.'

I took a sip from my glass of white wine, resolving to make it my last. I was just teetering on the edge of that nicely fuzzy-headed mellow stage and knew that any more might tip me over into the 'a-step-too-far' stage, and I wasn't sure Alex was ready for that. I gave him a sneaky sideways glance, hoping he might not notice, but our eyes met for a split second and a warm sensation filled my chest. Too late, I was definitely on the squiffy side of mellow now.

So I had no idea if Alex was a sophisticated hard-edged city type or a creative arty type, or more probably a compelling mixture of both. Whatever he was, and despite his dodgy views on marriage, I think I liked him. He had an air of authority about him, a quiet self-assurance that radiated from his body. A confidence that came from knowing he was good at what he did. He had an artist's hands too, I noticed; long expressive fingers that moved in an oddly compelling way as he spoke.

'What do you do then?' he asked casually.

I work in a garden centre.

The words caught at the back of my throat, refusing to come out. I'd never been embarrassed to say them before, so why I was hesitating now I didn't know. Instead, I opted for the glorified version, hating myself for doing so and wondering why I was even bothering. I mean, it wasn't as if I was out to impress Alex.

'I'm a buyer – luxury goods, gifts, for a large store.'

'Ah, okay,' said Alex, looking suitably satisfied with my answer. He had this weird way of nodding in silent approval when I answered a question, as though he was secretly interviewing me for a job, one I didn't know I'd even applied for. He was just about to ask me something else when Nana Gladys interrupted. She turned around, a big smile on her face.

'So can we expect you two lovely young people to be next?'

'Sorry?'

'Will you two be getting married next?' she said, just at the moment when a complete silence fell around the table and all eyes turned to look at us.

'Ah well,' said Alex, giving Gladys the benefit of his warm genuine smile. 'As much as that is a very tempting proposition, Jen and I have only just met today so I think it might be a little bit too soon to be talking along those lines, although you never know.'

A ripple of laughter ran round the table.

'What do you say, Jen?' He fixed his gaze upon me, his blue/green/brown eyes shining with mischievous intent and I looked away – not wanting him to see the flush of heat colouring my cheeks. He leant in closer, whispering in my ear. 'Weren't you just saying you thought that it might be a good idea?'

'Stop it,' I hissed, turning my attention back to Gladys.

'Oh, I'm sorry,' she said, laughing. 'Have I put my big foot in it?'

Admittedly it was hot in the restaurant, but now Gladys was blushing like a teenager, showing the tell-tale signs of a rush of heat spreading up from her neck to her cheeks. I'd only known

Alex a matter of hours, but I suspected he might have this effect on a lot of women.

'I could have sworn you two were a couple. You look so right together. Don't they make a lovely couple, Betty?'

'Yes they do. Very handsome. Lovely, in fact.'

Thankfully, saving us any more embarrassment, Angie and Tom were making signs to move at the other end of the table and the attention was deflected onto them where it should most rightfully have been.

It had been the most wonderful wedding breakfast. We'd had mouthwatering desserts of *croquembouche* and lemon posset, followed by a selection of continental cheeses. Angie's father had stood up and said a few words and if he'd harboured any bad feeling towards Tom then he certainly didn't show it. Tom gave a heartfelt speech which had most of the women in the room close to tears. He talked of his love for Angie and how he was the luckiest man on the planet to be given a second chance with the woman he wanted to spend the rest of his life with. No one in that room could have been in any doubt as to Tom's complete and utter devotion to his bride, or Angie's to her groom, as her eyes shone with love and affection.

'Thank you, darling, I love you so much,' Angie said, grabbing me for a hug, as the bride and groom went round the room saying their goodbyes.

'Oh, and I love you too! Have a fabulous honeymoon. Take lots of piccies. I need to see what paradise looks like.'

'I will, I will and I'll call you just as soon as I get back.'

In a shower of confetti, we waved Tom and Angie off as they climbed into the back of a waiting taxi ready to speed them off to the airport, and I was left with a funny feeling of regret, relief and happiness all rolled into one.

'Are you two coming back to ours for a cup of tea?' Even

Diane, Angie's mum, was getting in on the act now, talking to Alex and me as though we were a proper couple.

'That sounds like a lovely idea, thank you, we'd love to,' said Alex, putting an arm around my shoulder, answering as if we actually were one. Not that I minded in the least, it was just what I needed at the moment, a lovely cup of tea.

5

After three cups of tea, two shortbread biscuits, a slice of fruit cake, and a long and interesting chat with Gladys and Betty about Taylor Swift, her extensive back catalogue, her fashion high-fives and faux pas, plus the ins and outs of her love life which I knew nothing about but the sisters seemed to know everything about, I decided I really ought to go and do something to make myself useful. I rounded up some dirty plates and took them into the kitchen.

Alex was sitting on a kitchen stool, idly looking at his phone. He'd lost his jacket now and had rolled the sleeves of his shirt up, his tie loose around his neck. He looked relaxed and totally at ease, putting away his phone in his pocket when he saw me.

'So what time do you think the dancing starts?' he asked.

I laughed. His sense of mischievousness and fun shone in his eyes in a way that played havoc with my sensibilities. It had been a day of excess; the never ending glasses of champagne and wine had made me lightheaded, the delicious and abundant food had filled my tummy to the point where I thought I would never need to eat another thing again and the whole emotion of the occasion had made me thoughtful and fanciful. I glanced at my watch, it was definitely time to be going home.

'Ha, didn't you hear, the band have rung and cancelled. Looks like there'll be no dancing after all.'

'That's outrageous,' said Alex, shaking his head mockingly. 'What kind of wedding reception is this? Should I go and ask Gladys if she would do me the honour?' He smiled, looking up at me under long eyelashes, the faintest of dark shadows beneath his eyes lending him a vulnerability I hadn't noticed earlier. 'Look, I'm probably going to make a move. I could do with a livener, if I'm being honest. Do you fancy going back into town, finding a bar? What do you reckon?'

It was only a casual invitation, but I felt my heart flitter-flutter at the suggestion. At the same time Angie's cautionary words rang in my ears. This guy was a player, someone to be avoided at all costs, but despite knowing that and my head telling me I should really say my goodbyes and get the hell out of here, there was something about Alex that I found intriguing and compelling and, if I was being honest with myself, totally and utterly attractive. Totally and utterly not my type, but what did that matter. We were just two people who had hooked up together at a wedding and were enjoying each other's company. I wanted the excitement of the day to carry on into the night. I was fed up being a sensible Sarah. Mum would be urging me to be bolder, have more fun. It was almost as if I could feel her on my shoulder egging me on. The spontaneity that was missing in my life was now knocking at my door, beckoning me outside to play and that was a much more appealing proposition than the thought of going back to my empty flat with only the television for company. Besides, it was only a drink, it wasn't as if he was asking to marry me.

* * *

We ended up in a wine bar down by the river and despite my earlier protestations that I couldn't eat or drink another thing, as soon as I sat down and Alex suggested sharing a bottle of Prosecco, it was as if there was nothing more in the world I desired at that moment.

For a moment I felt a twinge of self-consciousness wondering what was I doing there and what we would possibly find to talk about, but I needn't have worried, Alex's confidence and easy charm put me completely at ease. I plastered on a big smile as he handed me a filled glass and I took a sip, the bubbles having an instant restorative effect.

'To Tom and Angie,' said Alex, raising his glass to mine. 'Wishing them all the best for a long and happy marriage.'

'To Tom and Angie!'

Alex's earlier comment came back to taunt me. I'd always had doubts about Tom as marriage material, or even boyfriend material come to that, but then I didn't know him nearly as well as Angie or Alex did. Was it really possible Alex knew something I didn't? Had he been trying to tell me that earlier? I couldn't bear the thought that there was something amiss, something I didn't know about. Or more worryingly, something Angie didn't know about.

'So, you never said,' I asked, trying for absolutely dead casual, really not bothered one way or the other, 'what chances do you give the happy couple for a long and happy marriage then?'

He gave me a rueful smile.

'I didn't think we were allowed to think along those lines. Look, I'm sorry if I upset you earlier, it was just an off the cuff comment. I didn't mean anything by it.'

'You do think it will work out for them though, don't you? I've never seen Angie looking so happy.'

'Yeah, well, I hope so,' said Alex, carefully avoiding my question and my gaze. 'Tom is a great guy. I guess they have as much chance as any other couple out there.'

'Hmmm.' I wasn't sure if Alex's lukewarm response was due to his reservations about Angie and Tom as a couple or if he was anti-marriage in general. I suspected the latter. 'Can you see yourself getting married one day?' I asked.

He tilted his head to one side, pondering on my question before pursing his lips.

'Possibly.' He tilted his head the other way, narrowing his eyes.

'Maybe.' He looked me directly in the eye.

'Definitely,' he said, laughing.

'Well, that's conclusive,' I said, laughing too.

'I don't know if I ever will,' I said, uncertain why I felt the need to tell Alex this riveting piece of information, and not realising I even felt that way until the words were out there.

'That's rubbish. I barely know you, but you strike me as the marrying kind. Here, let me have a look at your hand.' He took hold of my hand and turned it over, stroking his thumb across my palm. He pushed my fingers back and then gently traced the lines on my hand in a movement that was so light it was almost imperceptible, but still managed to send shivers down my spine at the same time. I looked up into his eyes and our gaze locked for the briefest moment, before I had to look away.

'Aha, just as I thought, I can see it all here, there's a very exciting future ahead for you.'

'Is that right?' I knew he was teasing me, but I was more than willing to play along with the game. 'So tell me then, what can you see?'

'Definitely a marriage. Within two years, I'd say. A big white wedding, I think.'

'Really, well I suppose I ought to get a move on and meet this mystery man then. Two years isn't that long to meet someone and then decide I'm going to marry him.'

'And your marriage will be blessed with children.'

'It will? Really? This is getting more interesting by the minute. How many?'

'Let me see.' He lifted my hand higher, peering closer at a random spot on my palm. 'Four, I'd say. Possibly more.'

'WHAT?!' I nearly snorted my wine out at that revelation. 'Four? Good grief. Absolutely no way. Two possibly, at the most, but there's no way I can imagine having four children. I'm not even sure I'm that maternal.' I snatched my hand away, laughing.

'Ah well, I find a lot of people don't want to hear the truth. It is a cross I have to bear with this special gift I have.'

'Is that so? Okay, tell me about my job then. Sounds like I don't need to worry about my personal life, that's all sorted, but I could do with some guidance on my career.'

'Let me see?' He picked up my hand again and ran his finger around the outline of my palm and then up and down and around the length of my fingers. By this stage I wasn't really bothered by anything he might have to say, I was more concerned about the magic his touch was tracing on my hand. That a touch so light could have such a startling effect on my whole being I found astonishing.

'A change is on the cards,' he said, adopting the croaky voice of an elderly woman soothsayer. 'You mark my words, young lady.' I laughed, shaking my head at him indulgently but he kept hold tight of my hand. 'Really,' he said, his voice back to normal now; warm, caressive, enticing. At that moment he could have told me anything and I would have believed him. 'I can see a lot in your future, but I'm afraid I can't really divulge any more. Not now. It will all become apparent with time.'

He dropped my hand like a hot potato.

'Oh.' I wanted to grab his hand straight back again and tell him not to stop. I'd been enjoying the sensations much more than I should have done.

'Sorry, but I don't want to put ideas into your head, you have to follow your own path without being influenced by anything I might tell you, but your fate is here, all laid out in your hand.'

'Right, well that's good to know,' I said, feeling flustered. 'Nothing I need to worry about then.' Heat flushed my neck and face. His attentions were far too distracting. I looked at my hand wondering if I'd missed something obvious there, all these years. I smiled and shook my head. 'Just one word of advice, Alex, don't give up the day job. I really can't see you ever making a career out of being a palmist.'

'Er, I hope you're not casting doubt upon my inherent abilities. People come for miles to have one of my special readings. Well, I'm sure they would if they knew what a special talent I have. I'll tell you what... do you have a pen... some paper?'

'No.' I raised my hands to the sky. 'I didn't think to pack any for the wedding. Silly me!'

Undeterred by my sarcasm, Alex beckoned the young waiter over. 'Excuse me! Do you have a piece of paper and pen I could borrow, please? And an envelope too, if possible?'

I looked at him bemused, wondering what on earth he was up to.

When the waiter had delivered the requested items, Alex started writing something down, craning his arm around the paper so that I couldn't see.

'What are you doing?'

'Oh ye of little faith. I'm just writing down one or two predic-

tions for you. You'll be able to look at these a year down the line
and think, "oh yes, that funny guy I met at the wedding, he did
know what he was talking about after all."'

'Can't I just read them now?'

'Nope. What's your surname?' he asked. When he finished
scribbling down whatever it was he was writing, he folded the
paper in half before inserting it into the envelope. He then wrote
on the outside.

*For Jen Faraday – Not to be opened, in any circumstances,
until one year from today's date.*

Then he proceeded to sign and date the envelope with a
dramatic flourish.

'But that's a whole year away!' I protested. 'You do realise I'm
going to go straight home after this and the first thing I'm going
to do is rip open the envelope and read what you've said.'

'No, you're not,' he said, removing the envelope from my
hand. 'Can't you read what it says? Not to be opened until this
date next year. And to save you from any temptation I'm going to
give this to the waiter and ask him to put it behind the bar with
strict instructions not to hand it to you until the designated date.'

'Really? You're mad, do you know that? Absolutely mad. I'll
have completely forgotten all about it by then. Memory like a
sieve, me.'

'Well, if that's the case then no harm done. But, if you do
happen to remember, and you're curious as to what's in here,' he
waved the envelope in the air, 'then you can always come and
have a look. In one year's time, that is.'

I laughed. Who knew where I might be then. Alex's predictions were probably as good a guess as my best surmising,
although I highly doubted I'd be married with four children!

'Well, thank you. You never know – if I'm in need of a bit of spiritual guidance in a year's time, I'll know where to come.' Although I suspected the barman would probably bin the note just as soon as the crazy, giggling and clearly drunk couple had left the building.

Alex was looking at me intently, a lazy seductive smile on his lips.

'Look, Jen. I don't want this party to end.' He reached across for my hand, but this time there was a very different intent in the action. 'Why don't you come back to mine for some coffee.' He pulled out his phone and tapped at the screen. 'Oh look, I've just had a text from the band.'

'What?'

'You know, the band who should have turned up at the wedding. They got their wires crossed apparently and turned up at my place instead.'

The breath caught in my throat as a tingle of anticipation ran down my arms.

A contented weariness spread along my body. It had been a lovely, but long and exhausting day. Weddings always affected me that way. Alex had been great company but I wasn't the type of person to go home with someone on a first date. Only this wasn't a first date and this wasn't just someone. This was a charming, gorgeous, red-hot date. Six months of trawling internet dating sites hadn't brought anyone of this deliciousness anywhere near my inbox. This was definitely the ideal opportunity to practice what my mum had preached and embrace my inner gorgeousness.

'Bloody band, getting the details wrong,' I said, leaning across to leave a small kiss of intent on his lips. 'I suppose we ought to give them the benefit of the doubt and turn up for at least one dance. I mean, it would be rude not to.'

6
_____

'Oh shit!' An arm hit me in the shoulder and a flurry of sheets and pillows and covers were tossed in the air as the slow realisation of where I was and what I had done filtered into my consciousness. 'Sorry, Jen, I've got an exhibition opening this morning. The artist is putting in an appearance and there's a whole host of guests turning up. Well, that's the plan anyway. I've got to go. I'm late as it is.'

Alex jumped out of bed without an inch of self-consciousness and I closed my eyes as though I hadn't seen him in all his naked gloriousness the night before. Slowly I opened them again, my eyes adjusting to the light filtering in through white linen curtains, my brain adjusting to where I was and hoping to God Alex wouldn't turn around again. Hoping that all of this was a product of my over-active imagination.

'Take your time though.' Oh God, there he went, doing exactly what I hadn't wanted him to do. I quickly snapped my eyes shut again, trying to somehow un-see what had just been staring me in the face.

It wasn't that I was a prude, it was just that I wasn't that sort of girl. Or at least I thought I wasn't until yesterday. I'd got to the ripe old age of twenty-seven and never had a one-night stand before. So lord knew what had possessed me to act so out of character last night and break a habit of a lifetime.

Possibly the champagne. Definitely the undeniable attraction of the man who was now running in and out of doorways, picking up and discarding various bits of clothing as though he was the lead character in a comedy farce.

What would Angie say if I told her? That despite all her warnings I'd ended up in bed with the groom's best friend. Probably best not to tell her, I reckoned. By the time she returned from her honeymoon this would all be a hazy memory.

A pretty good memory admittedly. Alex had been the perfect companion, funny, charming and totally seductive, and it had been all too easy to fall for his charms. Oh, and the dancing, how could I have forgotten the dancing. I'd felt like Ginger Rogers to his Fred Astaire – gliding around Alex's living room as though we could actually dance, laughing until we fell into an ungainly heap onto his sofa.

It had all felt so normal and natural, as if we'd known each forever, and now I sensed that late-night easy familiarity was about to be replaced by an early-morning awkwardness.

Alex was hopping about the bedroom looking less like the smooth operator of last night and more as though he had two left feet, pulling on a pair of black cotton boxers that only went a tiny way to making me feel any less embarrassed by being in close proximity to such a very naked man.

'Help yourself to tea or coffee in the kitchen. It's through there,' he pointed helpfully. 'There's cereal in the cupboard or some bread in the tin if you want to make toast.' He disappeared for a few moments before poking his head round the door again, only thankfully this time he was fully dressed. 'My phone's not over there, is it?'

I gave a cursory glance over the bedside cabinet. A radio/alarm clock, a pair of engraved cufflinks, a half dozen assorted coins but, more insistently, a pair of abandoned silver teardrop earrings that were flashing at me like a pair of Belisha beacons. I felt a wave of nausea. My gaze got stuck on those damn things until I realised Alex was waiting for an answer.

'Yep, it's here,' I said, leaning over and grabbing it for him.

'Cheers.' He came and perched on the edge of the bed and stroked his thumb across my cheek, taking the phone from me. 'I had a really great time yesterday, Jen. The wedding was fab, but sharing the day with you, getting to know you made it all the more special.'

I smiled, feeling vulnerable, naked under his bed covers while he was fully dressed. I resisted the urge to reach up and throw my arms around his neck, pulling him back into bed but I sensed a subtle shift in the atmosphere from last night. It was obvious he wanted to get away as quickly as possible.

'I've got your number so I'll give you a call. We can do it again, go out for dinner or something?'

I nodded, pulling the duvet up higher around my body.

'Or you give me a call, yeah?' he added.

'Yes, sure. We'll get something sorted,' I said, breezily. Now I remembered why I'd never had a one-night stand before. Everything that seemed so romantic and magical last night now only appeared sordid and awkward. Alex was going through the motions, saying what he thought was the socially acceptable thing to say in these situations, something he'd probably had a lot of practice at in the past.

He stood up and looked at his watch.

'Aargh, sorry, Jen, I would really love to stay, but I have to go.' He gave me a chaste kiss on the forehead before turning around and leaving. 'I'll see you soon, yeah,' he called, the front door slamming shut after his departure.

No sooner was he out of the way than I quickly jumped out of bed. I didn't want to hang around any longer than I had to, fumbling around his kitchen trying to feel as though I had every good reason to be there when in fact the opposite was true.

I'd felt a prick of shame even before I'd rolled out of bed, which was ridiculous really. I had absolutely nothing to be ashamed of. I was a consenting adult and so was Alex, although it didn't help that he'd already departed the crime scene. No, however much I tried to convince myself that this was all absolutely fine I still felt like a burglar stealthily negotiating a property I had no right to be in. I just hoped Alex wouldn't dash back and find me scrabbling around the floor for my knickers, or the doorbell wouldn't buzz or the phone wouldn't ring or the owner of the earrings wouldn't put in an early morning appearance. Those damned earrings! Who did they belong to exactly? I sighed. It had nothing to do with me, of course, but that was the trouble with romantic flings, there were so many unanswered questions.

I threw my clothes on, the ones so hastily abandoned last night, picked up my phone and my bag, gave a hasty check of the bedroom to make sure I hadn't left anything behind, before letting myself out of the front door, relieved and disappointed that I would never need to see Alex again.

* * *

I marched out of the wine bar, my cheeks stinging with humiliation. Damn that woman! Who the hell did she think she was, telling me I couldn't have my letter. I had every mind to march straight back in there and give her a piece of my mind. This time if she refused to hand it over I would clamber over the bar and rip it from her hands, but then if I did come off worst in a fight I might just be left with a few scraps of torn up paper which would defeat the object entirely. It even crossed my mind to phone the police to report the letter as stolen, but I could see that might be a slightly over-the-top thing to do. Besides, I wasn't entirely sure of my legal rights to an envelope with my name on, but with a 'do not open until' proviso scribbled across the front.

The thing was I felt even more curious as to the contents of that note this morning, although why I was tormenting myself with 'what-ifs' I didn't know. If I did get to read the letter, I would probably only end up disappointed. What was I expecting to find out? That Alex really did hold the secrets to my future. It was laughable. It had only been intended as a bit of fun.

That envelope was the only link I had with Alex now. Despite him saying he'd call me, I thought it was probably unlikely. Other than our mutual friends, Tom and Angie, we had absolutely nothing in common. The truth was I probably wouldn't see him again and that realisation as I mooched along the high street looking in the shop windows filled me inexplicably with a pang of sadness.

Crikey, what was wrong with me? I clearly still had too much wine sloshing around my veins to be making me so maudlin this morning. This was obviously why I wasn't cut out for this one-night stand malarkey. I was over-thinking the whole thing, giving it much more importance than it merited.

I stopped outside an employment agency and looked up at the myriad of jobs adorning the windows. At least I shouldn't have too much difficulty in finding some temporary work when I left Browns. Shame it wasn't open today or else I would have gone in and signed up, but I resolved to do that first thing tomorrow.

No, the best thing to do was completely forget about Alex. It had been great, but it had been of the moment and now the moment was over. Thinking about it, I don't suppose there'd even been an art exhibition he'd had to rush off to this morning – he was an accomplished one-night-stander and this was probably just his standard excuse for extracting himself from any awkward situations.

Ha ha, yes! If I was going to love more, with casual abandon, without losing my heart to every man who came along, I really would have to learn the rules of the one-night stand game.

I turned to go home, but something stopped me in my tracks. What was the point when I'd only end up slouching on the sofa watching a box set, while eating too much chocolate and drinking more wine which my body certainly didn't need. Much better to stay outside and walk off the excesses of the previous day.

I walked through the high street with a renewed sense of purpose, up into the Old Town and through the alleyways that were home to a selection of independent shops and galleries. I rarely came up here, I had no reason to, but there was no reason to say I couldn't. It was perfectly normal behaviour for a Sunday morning. Nothing out of the ordinary at all. It was what other people did with their weekends; strolled in the sunshine around the bespoke boutiques and jewellers, looking into the windows of the craft and gift stores, stopping off for a cup of tea or coffee in one of the many welcoming cafés.

My heart picked up a pace as I found Bell Alley and I walked along the cobbles on one side of the thoroughfare, my gaze scan-

ning the signs hanging above the shop frontages. When I saw
Woodland Studios I felt a sense of relief. It was definitely a
gallery and there were definitely people inside milling around
and yes, I just managed to see from the corner of my eye that it
looked to all intents and purposes like an art exhibition. Hooray!
Alex hadn't been lying to me after all. I could go home now with
my dignity and honour intact. I wasn't sure why it had felt so
important to verify that information, but it had and now my
curiosity had been sated I felt a whole lot better.

'Excuse me.' I was standing directly opposite the gallery
when a large man in a straw hat with a camera around his neck
stopped me. My eyes widened as I tried to circumnavigate his
considerable girth, taking tiny little steps one way and then the
other to try and hurry him along the path so that we were out of
direct sight of Alex's shop, but the American gentleman in the
hat wasn't picking up on my non-too-subtle hints.

'Yes,' I said impatiently.

'Sorry to trouble you, miss, but I wondered if you could tell
me where I might be able to buy some candy. I hear there's a
shop around here somewhere, but I've not happened upon it yet.'

My gaze did an involuntary sweep down to his rotund tummy
and I had to bite on my tongue to stop myself from suggesting
that perhaps he'd already had one too many candies. Instead I
smiled sweetly, and pointed him down the hill.

'Go down to the bottom of this alley and then turn right onto
Peacock Mews. The sweet shop is in the far corner.'

'Well, thank you, ma'am,' he said, tipping his hat towards me
in gratitude. 'You really are a perfect English rose, aren't you?'

'Thank you,' I said, blushing, using his considerable size to
hide behind as I shuffled round his body and attempted to make
my getaway before I heard a very familiar voice.

'Jen!'

I froze on the spot. Oh God no, please no. Not now. Let me fade into the background unnoticed.

'Jen, is that you?'

I considered for a moment asking the American if I could hide beneath his jacket and go and buy candies with him, but it was too late. I'd already been spotted. I peered out from behind the man to find Alex looking at me, a bemused smile on his face.

'Hey, I thought it was you. What are you doing here?'

I watched as the man sauntered off, a smile on his face and I wondered if it wasn't too late to run after him.

'Oh, me, I was, um, just walking home.' Humiliatingly I was still wearing my wedding outfit from yesterday which was looking as tired and past its best as I was feeling.

'But don't you live...' Alex screwed up his face, his brow furrowing. He pointed in the opposite direction to the way I was walking.

'Yes, but I thought I'd take the scenic route,' I said, laughing, trying not to sound like a mad woman. 'I needed a bit of exercise after yesterday.'

'Look, Jen,' he said, laying his hand on my arm and looking as though he might have got the assessment of my character very wrong. 'I'm sorry for not inviting you along to the exhibition, it just didn't occur to me. You're welcome to come in for a glass of wine now though if you'd like to.'

'Ah, thanks, but no. I'm late as it is,' I said, glancing at my watch. 'Another pressing engagement beckons. I'll just be on way.'

'Great,' said Alex, looking worried. 'Good to see you again. And so soon too.'

'Yep. Bye!'

I hurried off, my cheeks stinging an unbecoming beetroot colour, I felt sure. So now Alex would think I was a proper weirdo, stalking him after only seeing him a couple of hours earlier. What an idiot. I sighed, determined not to look back at the shop or the events of the last twenty-four hours. None of it mattered any more. It would be fine. I would just have to spend the rest of my life avoiding Alex Fellows.

7

Any shame or embarrassment I may have felt after that night spent with Alex was quickly forgotten about in the following weeks. It was a one-off thing, and while it had been lovely and memorable, it had now been consigned to history, even if Alex's compelling eyes came back to taunt me occasionally in the middle of night. I'd been busy in my spare time writing, taking photos and crafting, and really didn't have time for romance. There was only room for one man in my life at the moment.

It always lifted my mood to see Gramps' smiling, friendly face, and on that particular day I found him sitting in his armchair flicking through the pages of a travel brochure.

'Ooh, are you off somewhere nice, Gramps?'

'Well, I thought I'd go away, love, just for a couple of weeks. I've not been away since your nan died. It's about time, I reckon.'

'What a brilliant idea!' I called from the kitchen as I popped the kettle on. A few minutes later I brought in a couple of mugs of tea and two bacon sandwiches and sat down beside him. I peered over his shoulder and gasped, immediately taken in by the images of fairytale castles, mediaeval villages, towering mountains and dramatic scenery. A river cruise on the Rhine sounded right up my street. I don't know why it hadn't occurred to me before, but it made perfect sense to get away properly. I couldn't remember the last time I'd had a decent holiday. Angie and I had gone to Brighton for a long weekend last year, but that had involved a lot of cocktails, some frenetic dancing and some midnight paddling in the sea – so you couldn't really call it a proper holiday as we both came home feeling a whole lot worse than when we'd arrived due to the lack of sleep and our alcohol consumption.

No, a European tour would be just the ticket. Who wants to go and lie on a beach in the sun for a couple of weeks with a bunch of over-sexed girls when you can experience a bit of sophisticated culture with your lovely Gramps. I was definitely in need of some of that. I would meet new people, people I wouldn't necessarily meet otherwise, and it would give me the opportunity to dress up. I'd have to buy a whole new wardrobe especially, and I'd be able to sashay down to dinner in my new finery to eat seven-course meals. Who knew, I might even meet a handsome millionaire on the trip. At the very least it would give Gramps and me the chance for some special bonding time together too.

'Obviously I've got Harvey to think about.'

'How could we ever forget about you, Harvey?' I scooped up the little dog for a sneaky cuddle, fondling his ears. Already I was feeling so excited about this new turn of affairs. 'I don't suppose he'll like the kennels, but at least you know he'll be well looked after.'

'Oh, I couldn't put him in the kennels, love. That's the thing. I wouldn't be able to enjoy myself thinking of Harvey pining in a strange place. That's why I was wondering if you wouldn't mind looking after him while I'm away. He's no trouble, as you know, and he knows and loves you.'

'Me?' My voice came out as a squeak. Images of crystal-clear lakes, half-timbered chocolate box houses and black forest gateaux whizzed through my brain like the fast train. It clearly had no intention of stopping at my station.

'I think Marcia and I have decided on this one,' he said, holding up the page to me, the one I was now fully acquainted with, having been eagerly scanning it for the last few minutes. 'We can get a good last-minute deal on it.'

'You and Marcia?'

'Yes. Why? Oh, you didn't think...? Sorry, love.' He fell silent for a moment, concern on his features. 'Well, I'm sure you could come along too if you really wanted to. I could have a word with Marcia.'

'No! Oh God no! You wouldn't want me tagging along, cramping your style. Besides, you don't think I'd really want to go away with a couple of old fogeys like you, do you?' My tone was light, but my mood was as dark as the deepest recesses of all those Bavarian castles I wouldn't get to see now. 'Those sort of holidays sound like my idea of hell. Loads of people get food poisoning on those cruises, you know.'

I stood up, gathered the dirty plates and mugs, and took them through to the kitchen before returning and pacing the length of the living room. My gaze caught on a silver-framed photo of Nan, her deep blue eyes sparkling at me in understanding. Marcia and Gramps had moved onto the holidaying together stage already. Wasn't it a bit too soon for that? Did that mean they'd be sharing a bedroom, getting naked? Eugh. I blinked furiously, trying to rid myself of the scary images. 'Really, I couldn't think of anything worse.'

'Do you mean that?'

I sighed, tipping my head to the ceiling.

'No, I don't,' I said, slumping down onto the sofa. With my

legs stretched out in front of me, my bum slid down the edge of the sofa and I just stopped myself before landing in a disgruntled heap on the floor. Gramps looked at me from across the top of his glasses. He could always read me like a book.

'I would have loved to go to Germany with you Gramps, but Marcia, well, you know we would probably end up killing each other after a day or two.' I gave an evil chuckle.

'Oh, Jen. I do wish you'd give her a chance. She's not nearly as bad as you make her out to be.'

I rolled my eyes, feeling about fifteen again. For the last few years it had just been me and Gramps, and I liked it that way. Now Marcia was moving in on Gramps and it was as though he barely gave me a second thought these days.

'Well, it doesn't matter what I feel about Marcia. As long as you're happy, that's the main thing.' I stood, picked up Harvey and wandered over to look out of the window, burying my head in the dog's coat. 'Did you get rid of all Nan's things then?'

'Jen, don't be like that. I took some magazines to the tip and a few of her clothes to the charity shop, that's all. It has been four years, love.'

I shrugged, feeling an overwhelming and, what I suspected was a totally irrational, sense of betrayal. Things were changing all round me and I wasn't entirely sure I liked it.

'The thing is, Jen, I like Marcia a lot. She brings me out of myself and makes me feel young again. Is that such a bad thing? We're good friends. We get on well and have a laugh together, but she's never going to replace your nan. You do know that, don't you?' He eased himself up out of the chair to come towards me, but I dropped my gaze and turned away.

'Well, it's nothing to do with me. If it's what you want then that's fine,' I said. I put Harvey back down in his basket. 'Of course, I'll look after the dog while you're away.' I picked up my handbag from the floor and grabbed my coat. 'I need to get off, Gramps, or I'll be late for work. I'll see you later in the week.'

* * *

I guessed Polly Powers must be the work experience girl as, in all her natural adolescent beauty, she looked about fourteen. It wasn't until she sat down at the desk opposite me and straightened her pile of papers briskly on the desk, fixing me with a determined gaze, that I caught sight of the name badge on her lapel. *Polly Powers. Senior Recruitment Consultant.*

'Jennifer?'

'Yes. Hello.'

I looked across at her and smiled. With a name like that I half expected her to whip on her cape, twirl around on her seat and be transformed into a recruitment superhero with the means to find me the most perfect job in the world.

'Thank you for coming and filling out our application forms. I've had a quick scan through your paperwork, there's just a couple of things I want to go through with you, if that's okay?'

'Fine. Fire away.'

'I see you've been working for Browns... the garden centre, for nine years.' Her little nose crinkled when she mentioned the garden centre as though she wasn't entirely sure what one was. Or if she might get her perfectly manicured nails dirty merely by association. 'Can you tell me what sort of things you've been doing.'

'Well, a bit of everything really. I've worked on the tills, served in the restaurant, helped out in the nurseries tending to the plants, and worked in the office doing the accounts and admin. My most recent role has been sourcing stock for the gift and homeware sections. I like to think of myself as a bit of an all-rounder really.'

I'm not one to blow my own trumpet but when I said it like that it made me realise just how wide my range of experience actually was.

'So have you worked anywhere else then?'

'No.'

'I see. Do you have any spreadsheet, database, publishing experience?'

'Well, um, I like to dabble on the computer. I wouldn't call myself an expert but I can get by. I'm pretty fast on a keyboard.'

She raised her eyebrows and dug out a piece of paper from the bottom of her pile.

'The thing is, Jennifer, you didn't actually do very well in the typing test. I think you managed twenty-two wpm. For us to put you forward for typing or data entry work you would need a speed of at least forty-five wpm with an accuracy of ninety-seven per cent. Your accuracy was somewhat below the level.'

'Oh well, I only use two fingers to type, but once I get going usually there's no stopping me. It's just I'm not used to being tested and I was a bit nervous. I went wrong and then my fingers turned to jelly. Normally I'm much better than that. Should I have another go at the test?'

'We only allow three attempts and this was your best one.'

'Oh dear, was it? It was actually only temporary work I was looking for.'

'Yes, I appreciate that. The thing is, companies nowadays can take their pick of well-qualified applicants. Even for temporary work.' She looked again at my form. 'What about your accounts experience. Are you AAT qualified?'

'Am I AA... what?'

She sighed. I heard her. A small but very definite exasperated sigh escaped her lips.

'What about your waitressing skills? Silver service?'

I grimaced.

'I'm not entirely sure what that is, but it doesn't sound too difficult. Does it mean wearing a uniform and taking it very seriously? Not giggling? Not dropping anything? I'm sure I could pick it up pretty quickly.'

She paused and gave a big but not very convincing smile.

'Right. Well, I think that's everything.'

She tapped her papers on the desk again, signifying that this unsatisfactory meeting was coming to an end. The enthusiasm and positivity I'd felt only half an hour earlier when I'd walked into the employment agency had made an early exit without me. I wondered if Polly Powers' superpowers might be at a particularly low ebb today too.

'Thanks for coming along, Jennifer. If anything suitable comes along we'll be in touch.'

8

A memorial service for the late Arthur Cavendish
Headmaster of Hayward Upper School (between 1984 –2014)
will be held in The Priory, Dartington Road, Casterton
on Monday 22nd July at 11.00 a.m.
All who wish to celebrate his life are welcome to attend.

Feeling guilty about the way I'd behaved towards Gramps earlier in the week, I decided the best approach was to pretend we'd never even had the conversation about Marcia. Least said, soonest mended. I secretly hoped Gramps might tire of Marcia's busybody ways and their budding romance would fizzle out over a Bavarian beer and a bratwurst. After all, there'd be no greater test of their relationship than ten days spent in a small ship's cabin.

I dropped in on Gramps one day after work later that week and was just flicking through the pages of the local newspaper when I spotted the obituary.

'Oh, have you seen, Gramps? Mr Cavendish has died. My old headmaster.' I sighed, overwhelmed with sadness as I looked at the picture of Arthur Cavendish, standing tall and proud, a wide beaming smile on his face, just as I remembered him.

'What a shame. He was definitely one of the old school.' Gramps laughed at his own joke. 'A true gentleman, if I remember correctly.'

'He was lovely. Used to half scare the life out of me when he waltzed into the hall for assembly and his deep booming voice would ring around the room. Or he'd call me from along the corridor, "Jenn-i-fer Fara-day! Just. One. Moment. Please." Honestly, my heart would stop in my chest, wondering what I'd done, but most of the time he just wanted to chat. Think he must have kept an eye out for me because he knew Mum so well. She was forever on the phone to him.'

Gramps laughed at the memory.

'Well, your mum was always fighting your corner, Jen.'

'Yeah,' I sighed, suddenly transported back to my teenage years. My mum had been my best friend and staunchest ally back then. We'd had a really close bond, probably because it had only ever been the two of us since my dad left home when I was about five. At first he came to visit regularly but soon his visits dwindled away to nothing and Mum did everything she could to ensure she filled the gap created by his absence. It couldn't have been easy for her and I knew she worried when I went through the usual teenage traumas. I don't know how much she'd told Mr Cavendish, but he knew exactly who I was and always took a close interest in my progress in and out of school.

My gaze scanned the picture of that bygone time.

If Mum was still here, she would want to pay her respects to Mr Cavendish. More and more these days, ever since I'd re-read her letter, I felt her presence around me, giving me a gentle prod in the side, telling me what to do. And this was one of those occasions. I would take the day off work and attend on her behalf.

* * *

The sun shone high in the sky that Monday morning over the grounds of the priory as people filed in to celebrate the memory of a man who had dedicated his life to serving others. Not only was he a well-respected and much-admired headmaster, he was also a member of many local groups including the choir, the bowls club and many voluntary organisations too. I knew there would be a big turnout, but I hadn't realised just how many would be there until I found a seat and my gaze swept around the room and took in all the people, young and old, who filled the rows of the chapel. There were literally hundreds of them. Emotion caught at the back of my throat as a shiver travelled along my limbs.

'How did you know Arthur?' asked a lady in a purple hat who'd sat down beside me. I turned to her, smiling, grateful for the distraction.

'I was a pupil at Hayward School. I have very fond memories of Mr Cavendish. He was an inspirational man.'

'Oh yes, and a very kind and caring man too. I live in the same road as him and after my husband died, Arthur took on the job of mowing my lawns, front and back. I couldn't do it myself so I was always grateful to him for helping me out. I was just one of many people he helped. You can tell that by all these people here. He'll be sorely missed.'

The service was a joyous celebration of his life. Both his son and daughter stood up to read heartfelt eulogies to their father and his twelve-year-old grandson, who had a shock of blond hair, played a sonata on his flute which brought tears to my eyes and sent goosebumps down my arms.

When we stood up to sing 'All Things Bright and Beautiful' which seemed particularly apt with the sun's rays filtering through the stained glass windows of the chapel, I felt comforted and energised by the love and affection in the room for Mr Cavendish. I was reminded of my mum and nan too when a swell of emotion threatened to overcome me and I had to bite back the tears on more than one occasion. It was a warm and life-affirming service and I was so pleased that I'd been able to play a small part in it.

Outside, I was just saying goodbye to the lady in the purple hat when I heard my name called, a sound that sent a shiver of anticipation down the length of my body. Even before I had the chance to turn round I knew exactly who it was. Even after all that time. I'd recognise that warm, deep, seductive voice anywhere.

'Alex!' I said, turning to greet him with what I hoped was a confident smile. Inside, my heart was beating nineteen to the dozen.

'Jen, how lovely to see you.' He leant in and kissed me on the cheek and I caught a whiff of his scent, the same gorgeous smell that had so intoxicated me on the day of the wedding. Oranges, sun, sex. 'You look terrific. Did you go to Hayward school then? I didn't realise.'

'Yes. You too?'

'No, but my father was a good friend of his. They shared a passion for cricket and beer, and spent many a long lazy Sunday afternoon together putting the world to rights. My parents are abroad at the moment so I wanted to come along and pay my respects on Dad's behalf.'

He paused, with a smile, and I noticed the almost impercep-tible sweep of his gaze along the length of my body. I swallowed, feeling myself respond in a way that was totally inappropriate for what was supposed to be a sombre occasion, although I gave a silent prayer of thanks that I was wearing my black shift dress, heels and a coating of lipstick, and not my regulation Browns green sweatshirt.

'It was a lovely service,' I said, looking away, unsettled by his presence.

'It really was. Very moving.'

His gaze settled on my face and with it I was given a sharp reminder of the intensity of his eyes that were rocking a very definite green hue this morning. Whatever their colour, they were endlessly fascinating in their expression and warmth. I thought back to the night I'd spent in his bed and could hardly believe that I'd been so close and intimate with the man now standing in front of me. I knew him intimately and yet I didn't know him at all. If anything, he was much better looking than I'd remembered him to be when I conjured up his image in my head, which I'd done far more often than was healthy. Seeing him again made me realise just how much I'd missed him, if it were possible to miss someone you didn't actually know very well.

'How have you been?'

'Good.' I nodded. 'You?'

'Great.' There was a momentary pause. 'Do you have time for a coffee?' he asked, casually.

He was a man who looked good in a suit, the grey fabric – possibly silk, most definitely expensive – was perfectly tailored to show off his broad shoulders and trim waist. I glanced at my watch as though I might have an altogether more pressing engagement somewhere else.

'Yes, I've time for a quick one,' I said before I'd even considered whether it was a good idea or not. The only thing I knew was that I didn't want him to go, not just yet; anything that prolonged our time together had to be a good thing.

We fell into step with one another as though we'd done it a dozen times before and walked away from the chapel and through the streets of Casterton. It felt entirely natural being with Alex and ten minutes later we were tucked away in a corner of a quaint tea shop in Market Square. I was full of nervous antic-ipation, relieved to be able to sit down and have something to do with my hands, as I sat fiddling with the contents of the sugar bowl in front of me, but more relieved to be alone with Alex.

'There you go,' he said, when he'd collected two cappuccinos from the counter and brought them over to our table.

He also delivered two plates of cake, a vanilla slice and a coffee and walnut traybake which looked sinfully delicious and made me realise just how hungry I was. When he sat down he proceeded to cut both cakes in two and pushed the plates into the centre of the table. He gestured with a slight incline of his head for me to get stuck in. A man who definitely knew the way to this woman's heart.

'So how have you really been?' he asked for a second time, fixing me with a probing stare before picking up a piece of cake for himself and biting into it with gusto.

'Good, thank you. Busy.' I felt a heat warm my cheeks as our eyes met for a moment before we picked up our coffee cups in unison. 'The wedding seems like a long time ago now. What a lovely day it was.'

'It was.' There was a perceptible pause as his gaze roamed my face. 'I texted you. Did you get my messages?'

Not only had I received them, but I'd over-analysed them, obsessed over them, wondered if I should reply to them or if I should just delete the whole lot. I couldn't quite bring myself to do that. Instead I'd spent the last few weeks re-reading them, looking for any hidden intent behind his casual words.

Hi, just wondered if you fancied getting together for that drink? Let me know.

How are you? Hope all's well in the luxury goods world. Text me back when you have a mo.

Here's a sad face :(That's how I'm feeling right now. Thought you might want to get together some time, but I'm guessing not?

Am I being a pest? I don't mean to be, but would be great to hear from you.

Was it my bad dad dancing that put you off? I could take lessons if that would make a difference.

Or maybe it was my conversational skills, did I really bore you to death that day, and you were just being polite? Or maybe it was my aftershave? Hmmm, I've been thinking I should change it for a while now. Or was it perhaps my dodgy dress sense?

Not all of those things, surely?

Okay, let it not be said that I can't take a hint. You don't want to see or hear from me. I get it. Don't darken my doorstep ever again, kind of thing? It's deeply depressing, but I get it. If you change your mind then you know where I am :) x

'Yes, I did,' I said, feeling embarrassed now. 'I'm sorry I didn't reply, it was just...'

It was just what? I could hardly admit how humiliated I'd felt when he'd caught me loitering outside his gallery that morning. Every time I thought about it my cheeks stung with shame. I didn't want him thinking I was needy or just sitting at home waiting for him to call. It was a one-night stand. A pretty memorable one-night stand admittedly but it had served its purpose. It had proved that I could be witty and charming and attractive to men. In particular, a drop-dead gorgeous man like Alex. After being blind-sided by Paul, there'd been moments when I thought I would never date another man again.

Angie had warned me what sort of a man Alex was and so I'd decided there was no need for us to have anything to do with each other again. Just one night with him had left me feeling giddy, exposed and entertaining all sorts of fanciful thoughts. Any more and I knew I'd be in serious danger of getting in far deeper than would be good for my heart.

No, I'd decided to try the same approach with Alex as I had with Marcia. Putting it out of my mind. Pretending it had never happened. Only trying to forget about Alex wasn't nearly as easy as forgetting about Marcia.

Alex laughed, breaking the tension, holding up his hand to stop me.

'You don't need to explain.' He stirred his spoon around in his mug, tracing a trail through the creamy topping on his coffee, an action that was surprisingly distracting in its sensuousness. 'I think Arthur would have been pleased with his send-off today, don't you?'

'Oh yes, it was a wonderful tribute.'

Alex was thoughtful for a moment. 'Funerals always make you consider your own mortality, and that of your family and friends, don't they? I mean, we're all going in that direction one day.'

In the few interactions I'd had with Alex, I'd come to realise that he wasn't afraid of tackling some heavy subjects like marriage and death.

'I know.' I shrugged. 'Must admit I couldn't help thinking

about my mum and nan back there. It's the hymns, they always touch me deep down inside.'

'Oh, I'm sorry,' said Alex, reaching over for my hand, his fingers interlocking with mine, genuine concern in his eyes. 'I didn't realise you'd lost your mum.'

'Yeah, it was about eight years ago now and then my nan died a couple of years later. It was a difficult time, but in the end you just have to move on with your life. Somehow. It changes you though and you never forget those people who've played such an important part in your life. I always feel as though Mum and Nan are at my side.'

It was what everyone had told me at the time when I said I wasn't sure how I would ever get by without Mum. I didn't believe them when they told me I would. That I had to. That it was what Mum would have wanted. It was only now I was really beginning to appreciate that.

'Of course. Puts everything into perspective, doesn't it? And makes you realise that all those clichés spouted about life being too short are absolutely true. We definitely need to be making the most of the time we have here as none of us know how long we've got.'

I looked across at Alex. He still had his hand on mine, but it didn't feel awkward in any way. It felt perfectly natural, and a huge comfort too.

'Hopefully a little longer for both of us,' I said, with a wry smile. 'Enough time at least for me to finish my cake.' I dug my fork into the smooth mousse centre of the coffee and walnut slice and popped its gooey deliciousness into my mouth.

Alex looked at me indulgently. We were definitely bonding over the shared delights of the cake.

'If I died today, I'm not sure how many people would turn up for my funeral.' He tilted his chin upwards and narrowed his eyes, as though calculating the number of potential guests. 'Maybe sixty if I was lucky. There must have been about three hundred at Arthur's service. A reflection on what a great man he was and what a full and varied life he led.'

'Yes.' I screwed up my face to do the same calculation. 'Well, if it's any consolation I think there might only be about thirty people at my funeral so you're way ahead of me in the popularity stakes.'

Actually, it was a pretty depressing thought now he came to mention it.

'You know what we should do.' He lifted my hand in his, a big smile on his face. 'Start planning for our own funerals now. Widen our social circles, get more involved in the community, have a huge extended family, just so as we can be guaranteed a good turnout at our funerals.'

'Why are we even talking about this?' I asked, laughing. I really didn't want to be thinking that far ahead. Looking only six months or a year into the future was scary enough. I snatched my hand away from his, my fingers tingled from his touch.

He sat back in his seat, his eyes shining with mischievous intent.

'It is good to see you though, Jen. First a wedding and now a funeral, we seem to be making a habit of meeting at these big life-event occasions. Maybe next time we should do something a bit more low-key, meet for dinner or something?' He raised an eyebrow, a smile quivering at his lips. 'What do you reckon? Oh, I remember, you blew me out for dinner. Shame.'

I felt a heat rise in my cheeks and suddenly our corner of the tea room felt very claustrophobic. I shifted my gaze away from Alex and let it drift around the room, taking in the other customers; mainly yummy mummies meeting up for their morning coffee, singletons transfixed by their laptops and couples chatting away animatedly. A normal everyday scene, and yet here and now for me the scene was charged with an underlying fizzing electricity.

'Look,' I said, desperate now to clear the air. 'I'm sorry for not replying to your texts, I just thought... Well, I thought it would be better if...'

'Yes?' said Alex, chewing on the inside of his cheek, clearly relishing every moment of my obvious discomfort.

'Well, I thought it would be better if we just moved on and forgot that evening ever happened.'

'Oh right'. He chuckled and shook his head. 'It was that good, was it?' He crossed his arms in front of his chest, and his mouth grimaced in feigned umbrage. 'I know your type. Using me for your own personal ends and then just callously tossing me to one side when you've had your evil way with me.'

I was relieved he was laughing, but I still felt mortifyingly embarrassed. I hadn't expected to see Alex again, nor did I expect to have to explain.

Memories of the night spent in his deep double bed flittered into my mind. In truth, I'd thought of little else these last weeks; the way his deep intense gaze had devoured me, his warm seductive voice whispering in my ear, his touch on my skin taking me to peaks of delight I could only ever have imagined before. I knew I'd be playing with fire to go anywhere near this man again. Much better to avoid getting involved in the first place than having to piece together the fragments of a broken heart a few months down the line.

I'd set a precedent that night, falling into bed with him so easily, and there was nothing I could do to change that now.

'It wasn't like that. Look, if I'm being honest with you...' I looked over my shoulder to check no one was listening to what I was about to say and then I lowered my voice. 'That night I acted totally out of character. Honestly, I'm not sure what came over me. It might surprise you to know that I'd never had a one-night stand before.'

'Actually, that doesn't surprise me at all.'

'Oh.' Was it that obvious I was still wearing my 'L' plates as far as one-night stands were concerned? 'Well, don't get me wrong, I really enjoyed that day we spent together, and the evening bit, obviously,' I said, blushing. 'I was flattered that you got in contact and asked to see me again, but the thing is, I'm really not looking for that sort of relationship.'

Alex remained quiet for a moment, a quizzical look on his face. He ran a fingertip along an imaginary line on the table. I watched his hand as it traced a trail in front of me.

'And what sort of relationship would that be?' Alex asked, looking up at me.

'Casual sex,' I said quickly and rather too loudly, judging by the sideways glance from the man on the next table. 'I mean it was lovely and everything, and it's nothing personal against you, but I've realised I'm really not cut out for that sort of thing.'

'Ah okay.' I thought I saw the beginnings of a smile on his lips, but he bit it back. 'That wasn't what I was actually suggesting. I just thought it would be good to get to know you a bit better. I was thinking more along the lines of... dinner. You know, a proper date. It was just an idea though. I completely understand that you might not want to.'

Now I felt churlish and ill-mannered, but there was no getting away from the fact that Alex and I were completely different people with completely different needs. Hadn't Angie warned me that he was a serial dater and the last thing I wanted was to be the next name on his, no doubt, exceedingly long tbd (to be dated) list.

'I mean,' he said, now picking up my hand again and looking

deep into my eyes. 'I'm deeply hurt and disappointed at the thought that you might not want to see me again, but if that's the way you really feel, then what can I do.' He dropped my hand with a sigh. 'I'll just have to roll with that.'

He looked at me imploringly and I couldn't help my toes from curling and my mouth smiling at him in return.

'You know I went back to the wine bar to collect the letter you wrote to me.'

'You did!' His brow furrowed and his eyes darkened. 'Well, I do hope they didn't give it to you.'

'No, they didn't. I couldn't believe it. The girl was a right miserable bitch. All sour-faced and hanging on to that envelope as though her life depended on it. Honestly, I felt like slapping her.'

'Blonde hair, tall, skinny?'

'Yes, that's her.'

'She's a friend of mine actually. I'm glad to hear she was only doing her job properly.'

Oh God, why didn't that surprise me? Now I'd only gone and insulted his friend too.

'Look,' he said, laughing it away. 'Just take a chance, Jen. It's only dinner. Call it a one-off. If you hate it, and me, I promise you'll never have to see me again.'

When he put it like that I honestly couldn't see any reason to refuse.

'Okay,' I said, downing the rest of my cappuccino as though it were vodka, 'that would be lovely.'

'Really?' Alex's face lit up as though he hadn't actually believed I would consent. 'How about next Friday then?'

'Perfect!' I could be that girl who dated in a carefree and casual manner without losing my heart to the extremely good-looking man opposite me. I would just need to practice.

9

'Oh my god! What is that revolting smell?'

It was the first time I'd seen Angie in months, since the wedding in fact. She waltzed through my front door radiating good health; her hair was kissed with highlights from the sun and her skin was peppered with freckles, but there was something else about her too, an indefinable magical quality that made her look different somehow, changed in some way from the single girl I used to know.

She stopped in her tracks on her way down my hallway and took a deep inhalation. Her mouth curled in disgust, before she gagged and covered her mouth with her hand.

'Really, Jen, what is that stench? Has someone died?'

'It's my chilli jam bubbling away on the stove. I'm not sure what's happened actually. This is my third batch. The first lot I had to chuck out because it was too runny, the second lot was so thick you could stand a spoon up in it and this lot is smelling really vinegary. I'm not entirely sure where I'm going wrong.'

'Eugh, listen to you, Goldilocks.' Angie shuddered with distaste. 'So, what's with the domestic goddess stuff then?'

'Oh, it's for my new Insta account. I've only got a hundred or so followers at the moment, but I'm hoping to grow it over the next few months. I've been trying to put up a couple of posts a week. Seasonal gardening tips, simple craft projects, country kitchen recipes, that kind of thing. Molly from work gave me a jar of homemade chilli jam last Christmas and it tasted absolutely divine. I thought it would make a really popular post. How to grow your own chillies at home, making the jam and then decorating the jars for presents.'

'Blimey, you'll need to be careful not to kill off all your followers with that stuff. It smells like paint stripper.'

'You won't be mocking me when my jars of chilli jam are selling like hot cakes from garden centres across the country. I'll be the Paul Newman of Casterton.'

'Who the hell is Paul Newman?'

Honestly, Angie seriously worried me at times.

'The movie star?' I explained. 'Very handsome. Although sadly dead now. My mum was a huge fan. Anyway, he developed a range of salad dressings. They're sold in all the supermarkets. You must have seen them? Anyway, that will be me soon, although I think I probably need to tweak my recipe first.'

'Hmmm.' Angie raised her eyebrows doubtfully, before her shoulders heaved dramatically and she made a fist of her hand at her mouth.

'It's not that bad,' I said, laughing. 'Come in to the living room and I'll close the kitchen door. Fancy a glass of this?' I asked, taking the bottle of Prosecco she was offering. I kissed her on both cheeks, happy to have her back again.

'Maybe later. I could murder a cup of tea first, though.'

'So how was the honeymoon?' I asked, when I returned with our drinks. 'You've not really told me and I need a blow-by-blow account. You look amazing, by the way. Bronzed, radiant and just unbelievably happy. Married life obviously agrees with you.'

'Oh, it's fading already,' said Angie, holding her arms up for examination. 'We had such a brilliant time though, but honestly, even paradise can wear a bit thin after three weeks. All that sun, sea, sand and sex, it was exhausting!'

'Huh, chance would be a fine thing,' I said, pulling a disgruntled face.

'I've brought you this,' she said, handing me a pretty little gift-wrapped box. I quickly tore off the paper, opened it up and pulled out a green jewel encrusted bracelet.

'That's so lovely, thanks, Angie. You didn't need to do that, but I'm really happy that you did! It's so beautiful.' I giggled, fastening the bracelet around my wrist.

Settled on the sofa, Angie proceeded to tell me all about her honeymoon – showing me photos of their beachside villa and shot after shot of golden sands, blue skies and beautifully put together plates of food. It looked idyllic.

'Tom did some snorkelling and some paragliding. You know what he's like. He needs to get his adrenalin fix, but I was just happy to sit by the pool or on the beach, reading my book and dipping into the water occasionally just to cool off.'

'Sounds wonderful,' I sighed.

'Oh, it was. These last few months have been such a heady whirl. I have such lovely memories of our wedding day. I don't think it could have been more perfect. And to share it with the people we love most in the world, well, what more could we have asked for?' Angie let out a heartfelt sigh. 'So, did anything happen between you and Alex? Every time I looked over at you two, you were deep in conversation, gazing into each other's eyes.'

I laughed. 'I'm not sure about the gazing into each other's

eyes bit, but we had a great time. I'm really glad Alex was there to share the day with me. Yeah, it was good fun.'

If I'd been trying for nonchalant, Angie was having none of it.

'Good fun? Is that all? What happened after we left? Did you two go on somewhere? Was there any schmoozy-moozy stuff going on that I should know about?'

'No, don't be daft. We just went for a quick drink to round the evening off. It was lovely, really nice.'

Angie and I didn't have secrets from each other, or at least we hadn't up until now, but I wasn't going to admit to her or to anyone else, come to that, that I'd gone home with Alex that night. I barely liked to admit it to myself. Just the thought brought me out in a hot prickly rash. Besides, Angie had Tom to confide in so it was perfectly reasonable that we wouldn't share absolutely everything with each other any more.

'He's been asking after you, you know?'

'Who has?'

'Alex, of course!' said Angie, looking exasperated. 'He was saying to Tom what a great girl he thought you were and how much he enjoyed your company. I think he was trying to find out if there was anybody else on the scene. If you were available?'

'Really?' I looked away, not wanting to meet Angie's eagle-eyed gaze, the hot prickly sensation putting in a reappearance. Funny, I thought I'd had 'available' plastered all over my fore-head. 'Well, I do hope Tom didn't give away all my deepest secrets.'

'Well, you know Tom. He's pretty clueless when it comes to these things so I think your secrets are safe with him. Do you think you'll see him again?'

'Alex? He's texted me a few times, but I don't know that I will.' I didn't enjoy lying to Angie, but to be honest I still wasn't sure if I'd done the right thing in agreeing to a date. Half of me was still thinking I might cancel. 'Don't get me wrong, he's a great guy, funny and charming and good-looking, but...'

But what? If I'd heard anyone else describing a single available man that way I would have rushed over and nabbed him for myself. What was it that was stopping me from seeing someone I actually really liked? Alex was the first guy I'd fancied in ages, so why couldn't I just roll with it. The trouble was – it wasn't only the fact I fancied the pants off Alex, there was more to it than that. We'd clicked in a way that rarely happened with other guys; there was a connection between us that I'm sure I hadn't imagined. One I couldn't put down solely to the number of glasses of wine we'd drunk that day either.

'...we're different people,' I managed to conjure up. 'And he's really not my type.'

'Well to be honest, I'm pleased,' said Angie, sounding relieved. 'I was worried he might have cast you under his spell. You wouldn't be the first or the last. From what Tom's told me, he's bad news as far as women are concerned. P-L-A-Y-E-R. Big time. Commitment issues too, I think.'

If I'd been wavering, Angie's damning assassination of Alex's character had definitely put paid to any doubts.

'Sounds like I did well to escape his clutches then,' I said, breezily, trying hard to hide my disappointment.

That was the issue. It had been almost too easy being with Alex; the conversation had flowed smoothly, along with the wine, and falling into bed with him had seemed like the most natural thing in the world. A one-off, never happened to me before kind of thing, but I was realising it was much more of a regular, everyday kind of thing for Alex. Did I really just want to be another notch on his bedpost?

As soon as Angie went home I'd send Alex a text cancelling our date.

'Anyway, I'm going to have a top-up,' I said, picking up my empty glass. Best to forget all about it and move on. I brought the bottle of wine in from the kitchen. 'Are you ready for one?'

Angie shifted on the sofa, tucking her legs beneath her.

'Um, do you have something soft, a coke or a lemonade?'

I looked at her askance. The girl who could drink me under the table and still come up smiling was asking for a lemonade. If this is what married life did to you I wasn't sure I wanted any of it.

'Oh my god,' I cried, in a blinding moment of realisation, almost dropping the bottle in surprise. There could only be one reason for Angie being off the booze. 'You're pregnant!' I said, accusingly, dropping back down on to the sofa.

She nodded, her eyes widening. A smile spread across her lips as her cheeks flushed pink.

'Yep. Can you believe it? It wasn't planned. It just happened.' Angie held her hands up to the sky as though it was one of life's mysteries. 'It did mean I spent most of the honeymoon throwing up but I always think if you're going to be ill then it's much better to do that in paradise.'

'Oh darling, I am so happy for you both. That's the most amazing news.' I stared at her stomach as though seeing it for the first time, as though it had taken on a life force of its own, which it had! I pulled her towards me for a hug, surprised to feel tears gathering in my eyes.

She'd always said that she hated children and swore that she would never have kids of her own, but here she was pregnant with her first child. Angie would make the most wonderful mother. It just amazed me that it had never occurred to me before.

'I couldn't be happier. It's all been a bit crazy, first the wedding and now this. Funny how your life can turn around so quickly.'

She was absolutely right there. This time last year we'd both been single girls about town without a care in the world. Now she was married and expecting a baby, and had a whole heap of responsibility on her shoulders. It certainly explained why I noticed the subtle change in her appearance; radiant, happy and tired all rolled into one.

'What does Tom think?'

She screwed up her face and winced. 'He was completely shocked at first. It wasn't planned and I think he would have liked more time to ourselves before we started a family, but events have been taken out of our hands now.' She shrugged, looking as though she couldn't quite believe the news herself. 'He's slowly coming round to the idea though. He's going to be the best dad ever.'

'And you're going to be the best mum ever. I just know you are.'

'Do you know,' said Angie, looking thoughtful. 'This just confirms to me that it was all meant to be. It's as though fate has stepped in and decreed that this would happen. Do you believe in fate, Jen?'

I pondered on that one for a moment. Had it been my fate to spend nine years with Paul, thinking we would end our days together only for him to have a complete change of heart at the last moment? 'I don't know.'

'I do. I know it sounds daft, but I'm a great believer in these things. Tom and I were always meant to be together, he just needed a little convincing of the fact.'

She giggled, and I thought that I'd never seen her looking happier.

'Well, I think it's the most brilliant news.'

Obviously Fate was far too busy sorting out Angie's love life to step in and do something about mine, but I was hopeful that my turn would be next. Perhaps Fate just needed a nudge in the ribs, a reminder that I was here, ready and waiting. Perhaps if I put out a small request to the universe, they'd be able to do a job lot and sort out my love life and everything else at the same time.

Thinking about it, perhaps I didn't believe in fate after all.

'Jen?'

'Yeah?'

'Sorry to go on, but your chilli jam, do you think it's all right out there?'

'Oh shit!' At that moment the aromas of burnt sugar and vinegar so pungent it hit me right in the back of my throat, making my eyes water, wafted out to join us in the living room. I dashed out to the kitchen, grabbed a tea towel and snatched the stock pot off the hob, peering hopefully into the pan. I stuck my wooden spoon into the gooey black flecked mess and attempted to give it a stir, but that congealed blob of sugar wasn't going anywhere.

'Hmm,' said Angie, looking over my shoulder, giving me a reassuring squeeze with her hand around my waist. 'If you want my advice, darling, that recipe needs a little more tweaking.'

10

It was my final week working at Browns and by Thursday I'd cleared all my paperwork and drawn up lists of the jobs I did on a daily, weekly and monthly basis for my successor. I prepared spreadsheets, updated my filing systems and transferred the huge pile of business cards on the office desk onto the contact lists on the computer.

There was still a part of me that felt guilty about leaving Matt in the lurch, but there would never be an ideal time to leave and I'd stayed longer than I'd intended to, seeing out the busy summer period. Everyone at work had expressed their surprise when they'd learnt I was moving on. Matt had called me his right-hand woman and wondered how he would ever manage without me. A couple of times he'd asked if there was anything he could do to make me change my mind and had offered me considerably more money and a new role within the company to entice me to stay, but I knew if I didn't leave now, I never would. I'd be collecting my pension from Browns.

With nothing left to do in the office that day I picked up my gloves and headed outside to the nurseries. I wasn't a natural horticulturist, but there was always something that needed doing in that department and after a quick word with Tim, the manager there, he pointed me in the direction of a pile of compost that had been spilt over by the hebe display.

It was one of the things I'd loved about the job, the variety. If things ever got too intense in the garden centre or in the office I would come outside, get away from the crowds and find something to do with my hands. The fresh air cleared my head and being close to nature, feeling the soil beneath my fingernails, gave me a different perspective on whatever it was that was troubling me.

It was one of the things I intended to focus on in some of my online posts, the mental health benefits that came from gardening, whether you had a couple of acres to tend or just a small window box. It could be hugely therapeutic to be at one with nature.

I found myself a broom and began sweeping up the compost scattered over the floor, mulling over the fact that I had only two more days to go before I left Browns for good. In some ways I could hardly believe it. It was definitely the end of an era, but hopefully the beginning of a new one too. I hoped I wasn't making the wrong decision. I was sure I wasn't, but I supposed it was only natural to have the occasional wobble. I was just mentally preparing a to-do list when I became aware of someone standing to my side watching as I manoeuvred the broom across the floor.

'Sorry,' I said, turning around and resting my hands on top of the brush, 'can I help you at all?'

'Yes, I hope so.'

'Oh my god! What are you doing here?'

Alex, who was beginning to make a habit of turning up when I least expected it, was standing in front of me, that familiar seductive wide smile on his lips. He was wearing smart navy chinos, a white shirt unbuttoned at the collar and brown brogues. He didn't look like your average garden centre customer and I was reminded, with a heart-thumping jolt, of just how heart-piercingly, knee-bucklingly good-looking he was.

'Is that how you speak to all your customers? Or is that tone just reserved for your special ones?'

'I'm so sorry,' I said, quickly trying to cover up my shock. 'I didn't mean to be rude, it's just a surprise to see you here.' I ran a hand through my hair and felt a shower of compost fall onto my face. I wiped it away with the back of my hand. It had been a long week, I had no make-up on and was wearing my old and unflattering company sweatshirt which did such wonders for my colouring. I realised I must look a complete and utter mess.

An amused expression spread across Alex's face as though he was thinking exactly the same.

I attempted to channel my inner gorgeousness but I suspected it had already packed its bag and left for home.

'Was there anything in particular you wanted, something I can help you with?'

Perhaps he wanted a new conservatory, a lawnmower or a set of garden gnomes, although to be honest I couldn't really imagine any of those things featuring in Alex's lifestyle.

'I wanted to see you, Jen. That was all.' His voice was low and caressive. 'Tom mentioned you worked here and I was just passing so I thought I'd drop in.'

'Oh...' So my cover as a high-flying retail buyer was blown. General garden centre dogsbody it was. 'Oh... well, that's great. It's good to see you again.'

'Is it? Really?' He inclined his head, the corner of his mouth curling in doubt.

He honestly didn't know how good it was to see him. My

whole body had gone into overdrive; my heart was pounding in my chest, the hairs on my skin were standing to attention and every nerve ending in my body tingled in anticipation. I was only relieved I had the broom to hang onto. It gave me something to do with my hands and stopped me from falling over which would have been entirely possible the way I was feeling right now.

I nodded.

'Must admit I was disappointed when you cancelled on me, Jen. I was so looking forward to our date and then when you didn't take my calls... I just wanted to know, did I do something to upset you?'

'No, nothing like that.' I felt a heat rise to my cheeks. How could I possibly expect Alex to understand the way I felt when I could barely make sense of it myself. I spent every waking moment thinking about him, fantasising about some kind of future together and yet I knew deep down there could never be any future for us beyond a few hot and heady nights.

I wanted much more than a man like Alex could ever offer me. As it was, I'd spent far too much time obsessing over what he was doing, who he was doing it with or if the owner of the earrings hadn't moved straight back into the warm space I'd vacated in his double bed.

I wasn't cut out for the uncertainty and thrills and spills that knowing Alex had already brought to my world. Much easier to pack that whole episode away in the box, the very small box called one-night stands, and never have to visit it again.

'Sorry, I meant to text you back, but I've been busy. I'm leaving here tomorrow so it's been hectic.'

'Really? Where are you going?'

'I've got a few different plans. Ultimately I want to set up my own business, but in the meantime I'll be doing some freelance work.'

It all sounded a bit vague even to my own ears.

'Sounds great,' Alex said, being polite, I suspected.

We fell silent for a moment, Alex seemingly fascinated by my broom which was making me feel more like Cinderella by the moment, and me by the realisation that here was a man who didn't know how to take a hint. Why was he still here? Why hadn't he moved on to the next conquest on his list? What was it he wanted exactly? Was he so unused to being knocked back that he saw me as a challenge now?

'Everything okay?'

From out of the shadows Matt had appeared, a warm smile on his face, but I'd known him long enough by now to recognise that cold glint in his eye.

'Absolutely fine, thank you,' Alex said. He leant forward, making a show of reading the name off my badge, 'Jen... here... is giving me advice on some floating plants for my pond.'

I bit back a smile. What I knew about floating plants you could write on the back of a postage stamp. Matt would say I knew even less than that, I suspected.

'Okay. I'll leave you in the hands of our resident expert then, but if there is anything else you need,' he said, looking at me, 'then you know where to find me.'

I squirmed with embarrassment as my boss wandered away.

'What are you doing tomorrow after work?'

'Um...'

'Good. How about I take you out to dinner to celebrate your last day at work?'

My brain wasn't working fast enough to come up with an appropriate excuse, although I suddenly realised I didn't want to find one. In the flesh, up close and personal, Alex was much more difficult to resist than when he was at the end of the phone. With it being my last day tomorrow I already had that end-of-term feeling and the prospect of going out to dinner with a frankly too-sexy-for-his-own-good art gallery owner was much more appealing than going back to my empty flat.

'That sounds—'

'—brilliant.' He didn't even give me the chance to finish my sentence, but I might have opted for the same word in the circumstances. 'I'll pick you up at seven thirty then. How does that sound?'

He kissed me on my cheek, right there in the middle of the herbaceous perennials, sending a thrill of longing through me that I wouldn't normally have associated with flowerbeds.

It sounded pretty good to me. I looked around, flushed with excitement, wondering if anyone had noticed our public display of affection. I wasn't surprised to see Matt over on the other side of the nurseries scowling, unable to hide his displeasure. Perhaps it was just as well I was leaving tomorrow after all.

11

That night, after work, I was on my way round to see Gramps when my mobile buzzed in my pocket. I pulled the car over to a safe spot on the side of the road, before answering the call.

'Hello, sweetie,' breezed Angie's voice down the line. 'Don't suppose you're free tonight? Seems like ages since we've had a proper chinwag. Fancy some sparkling wine and a couple of DVDs?'

'Umm, you're not allowed fizz in your condition, remember?'

'Sparkling apple for me, but I have some of the proper stuff for you. We could have a cheeky look at some of those dating sites, if you want. I could do with a giggle. I like to keep abreast of what's new on the market, even if I'm no longer in a position to buy.'

'Oh, I'd love to, Angie,' I said, laughing, 'but I've got a red-hot date tonight, so won't be able to make it.'

'Really? Oh my god! Why didn't you tell me?' Angie's excitement fizzed down the line. 'Who is he? It's not Alex, is it?'

'Actually he's a very distinguished older guy. Suave, charming and very eligible.'

'Squeeeeee.'

I laughed. 'Oh Ange, don't get too excited, it's only Gramps. I'm surprising him by popping round and cooking dinner. A celebratory meal to mark me leaving Browns tomorrow.'

'Oh, you tease! You honestly had me going there, but aren't you the perfect granddaughter? That's such a lovely thing to do.'

I unclipped my belt and loosened my tensed shoulders into the back of the seat, wondering if I'd imagined a note of wistfulness in Angie's voice.

'So how's married life?'

'Just peachy. Well, it might be if I got to see my husband occasionally. I'm usually asleep in bed by the time he gets home at night.'

'Oh, that's tough.'

'Yeah, I just hope it won't be like this when the baby arrives. I know Tom has to put in the hours for his job, but it would be nice to have a bit more time together. I suppose I'm just feeling a bit deflated after the wedding and honeymoon.'

'Welcome back to reality, darling! Have you spoken to him about it?'

'No. I'm trying hard not to appear needy and clingy. He always hated that before. It was one of the things we argued about. I know Tom's career has to come first. It's only now, with the baby on the way, I've realised how hard that is at times.'

'Yes, but it should be different now, Angie. You're married. Tom must appreciate that both your lives have to change in some way. He has to compromise as well as you.'

She hadn't said as much but I suspected the after work drinking sessions which had always played such a big part in Tom's city career were still very much in evidence.

'Oh, don't mind me, I'm just having a whinge. I'm feeling fat, spotty and unloved at the moment.'

'It's only your hormones,' I said, sounding like I knew what I was talking about. 'But honestly, Ange, you should lay down a few ground rules. Talk to Tom. Get him to agree to a couple of nights a week when he makes an effort to get home at a reasonable time. It isn't a lot to ask for.'

'Yeah, you're right. Besides, I'm sure everything will fall into place once the baby arrives.'

I wasn't so sure about that and was still thinking about my conversation with Angie when I pulled up outside Gramps' bungalow. I had my doubts as to whether married life would change Tom or if he wouldn't just carry on in the same way as he'd always done.

Still, she'd known better than anyone what she was letting herself in for. And she'd told me they'd smoothed all those problems out so I hoped I was just worrying unnecessarily.

I climbed out of the car and retrieved my shopping bags from the boot.

'Hi Gramps,' I called moments later, letting myself in through the back door. 'It's only me!'

'Hello, love.' I walked into the kitchen but it wasn't Gramps greeting me, it was Marcia – she was standing at the stove tending to a frying pan that was emitting the most wonderful aroma of rosemary and garlic.

'Oh,' I said, unable to hide my surprise and disappointment at finding her there.

'I'm just making your Gramps some liver and bacon, I've got some sauté potatoes in here,' she said, shaking her pan, looking like a proper Mary Berry, 'and some new season asparagus ready to go. It's his favourite meal, but he tells me he hasn't had it in years.'

I looked over at the dining table that had been transformed by a white linen tablecloth with a pretty pink tea-light holder shining softly between the two place settings laid. It looked lovely and Marcia had clearly dressed for the occasion in a floral floaty dress and a pair of strappy sandals.

'That's nice,' I said, wondering why I hadn't known about the liver and bacon thing.

The dine-in for two ready meal of coq au vin, with chunky chips and garden peas, with a dessert of rich chocolate torte, hung heavy in the plastic bags I was carrying in my hands. I considered whipping them away and taking them home with me, but eagle-eyed Marcia had already spotted them.

'So, what have you got there?' she asked me, as Gramps wandered into the kitchen. He was wearing a pair of tan corduroys and a pink and white striped shirt, clothes I'd never seen before. He looked as though he'd just walked out of the pages of a catalogue for the older man. I suspected Marcia might be behind the fashion overhaul too.

'Hello, love.' Gramps hugged me. He even smelled differently these days. Fresh and outdoorsy. 'This is a lovely surprise,' he said, laughing as he pulled away, ruffling my hair with his hands. 'To what do we owe this pleasure?'

'I didn't realise I needed an invitation to visit my own granddad?'

'Don't be silly. Of course you don't. It's just...'

'I brought you a couple of bits,' I said, handing over the carrier bags.

Marcia took a peek into the bags over Gramps shoulder.

'Ooh look, Harry, there's a lovely bottle of wine in there. And a couple of delicious looking desserts too. We could have those after our dinner. How very thoughtful of you, Jennifer.'

'They're not for you, Marcia,' I said sharply, turning my back on her. 'I was going to cook for you, Gramps. To celebrate the fact that it's my last day at work tomorrow, but never mind. I can see you've made other plans.'

'Oh, what a shame. You should have told me and then we could have got something sorted. Why don't you stay and have some dinner with us? I'm sure there's enough to go round.'

'Of course,' said Marcia, feigning delight, but I wasn't fooled by her skills as an actress. I'm sure her dislike of me was every bit as strong as my dislike for her.

'I hate liver and bacon,' I snapped. 'And besides, I thought roast beef was your favourite meal?'

When had I ever had to give Gramps prior notice before? I often turned up unexpectedly after work and whipped up a quick bowl of pasta for our tea. Tonight was meant to be special, but Marcia had put paid to that.

'You can have a couple of favourites,' said Gramps, trying to appeal to my better nature. 'Tell you what. Let's do it tomorrow night then. I'd like that.'

'No, I can't. I've made other plans. I wanted to do it tonight, but it really doesn't matter now.' I sounded churlish to my own ears, but I couldn't help myself. It felt as though it mattered much more than it should have done. 'I should go. Leave you to your romantic dinner *a deux*.'

'Jen, I...' Marcia started, but I didn't want to hear anything she might have to say.

I slammed the door shut behind me on the way out, biting on my lip to stop the tears that were threatening to fall. On the way to the car, I pulled out my phone from my pocket and tapped on Angie's name.

'Hi darling!' She answered almost immediately.

'That offer for wine, does it still stand? I've been blown out by my date tonight. He's only gone and found himself another woman!'

'What? Bloody hell! Men, eh? You can't rely on any of them. Come on over, I'll have a glass of chilled fizz ready and waiting for you.'

12

'Oh my goodness, look at all this!'

I walked into the garden centre restaurant the next day at lunchtime, intending to pick up a sandwich and a cup of tea like I did most days, to find the rear of the restaurant cordoned off with pink ribbons. Chequered bunting and bows were festooned from the ceiling and brightly coloured balloons bobbed from the backs of chairs.

A huge cheer went up as I walked in and I was quickly buried under a flurry of hugs and well wishes from all my friends and colleagues. Champagne corks popped as Frank, one of Browns' longest-serving employees, broke into a spontaneous rendition of 'For She's a Jolly Good Fellow' which everyone else quickly joined him in.

I looked all around at the familiar faces gazing at me with affection, and felt overwhelmed by the warmth of their welcome. Someone handed me a glass of prosecco and a tray of delicious canapés was wafted under my nose. I took a salmon mousse topped blini and stuffed it in my mouth in an attempt to stop the unexpected surge of emotion at the back of my throat from escaping.

Matt greeted me with his customary wide smile and enveloped me in a huge bear hug, before stepping backwards to hold me at arms' length.

'Well, you didn't really expect us not to mark your last day with Browns in some small way?'

'This is lovely, Matt. Thank you. Really, I'm going to miss this place so much and everyone in it.'

'Well, you do know it's not too late to change your mind. Your replacement is due to start Monday morning, but I could always ring her. Tell her not to bother coming in.'

I laughed, but I suddenly felt overwhelmingly sad inside. This place had been such a huge part of my life for so long and now I was leaving it all behind. All the time I'd worked for Browns I'd felt safe and protected and now I was heading out in the big wide world to a new adventure, and however much that inspired and thrilled me, it also terrified the life out of me.

'Great though that you've found someone for my role,' I said brightly. At one time I would have been privy to everything Matt was doing, but I hadn't even known he'd been interviewing people, let alone hired someone. I knew he'd been holding back until he was certain that I was actually leaving and didn't have a last-minute change of mind.

'Yep, she seems like a great girl. She reminds me a lot of you, actually. She's only twenty, but she's very ambitious, full of enthusiasm and she's got a lot of great ideas for moving the department forward.'

'She sounds perfect,' I said, feeling a stab of pain to my stomach. It was funny to think someone else would be stepping into my shoes, doing the job I'd loved doing for so long, forming a close bond with Matt.

'Well, I don't suppose she'll be anywhere near as perfect as you are, but I'm sure we'll muddle through without you somehow.' He put an arm around my shoulder, genuine affection shining in his eyes. 'Besides, I'm sure we haven't seen the last of you, Jen. I'll be expecting you to pop in every now and then to keep us updated on all your news.'

'Oh, I will do, don't you worry about that. And I'm going to be mentioning Browns at every opportunity I get. In any social media posts or articles that I get published. I'm hoping to do some product reviews too so expect a huge influx of sales from my recommendations.'

'I will do, Jen,' he said, solemnly. 'I'll hire in some extra staff to cope with the sales rush.'

I smiled as he dashed back onto the shop floor to sort out a problem with the tills, which was something of a relief. It gave me a chance to get my fluctuating emotions under control. One minute I was laughing, the next I was close to tears. Home time couldn't come a moment too soon today.

'Hello, lovely girl,' said Molly, filling the space recently vacated by Matt. 'Do you know, Jen, I'm still so sad that you've decided to leave Browns. It won't seem right without you about the place. I thought you'd be like me, Jen, collecting your pension from Browns.'

I sighed, looking into Molly's lovely warm sparkling eyes.

'Well, there was a time when I thought so too, but I'd got to that stage where I felt desperate to move on. I needed a change. It wasn't only the job, it was lots of other things going on in my life too. And it was a case of if I don't do it now, then I might never do it. Have you ever felt that way, Molly?'

'Not really.' She shrugged, as if she had no idea what I meant. 'Every day I've spent working at Browns has been a happy one and I can't think of any company that I would have preferred to work for. It's natural to think the grass is greener somewhere else, but it isn't always the case.'

'I suppose,' I said wistfully.

'And I hope I'm not speaking out of turn here, but I always hoped you and Matt might have a future together, you know, as a couple.'

I laughed, and turned to look at her sharply.

'What ever made you think that?'

'I don't know. You just seem to go well together. And he always lights up whenever you're around.'

'No!' I said, feeling myself blushing. 'Matt and I have only ever been friends. We work well together as a team, I admit that, but that's as far as it goes, I'm afraid.'

'Ah well, perhaps it was just wishful thinking on my part, but you never know – funnier things have happened,' said Molly, a mischievous grin on her face.

My gaze drifted across to the other side of the room where Matt was now chatting in his usual animated style to a couple of the team. I wondered if there could be any truth to Molly's words. I'd always known Matt had a soft spot for me, but I'd put that down to the fact that he'd felt sorry for me when my mum died and had taken me under his wing. It couldn't be more than that, surely? Although the way he looked at me yesterday when I was talking to Alex might suggest otherwise.

Now, observing him across the room, it was like seeing him for the first time. He was good-looking in anyone's book. Not in the same jaw-dropping head-turning way as Alex, but in a more natural guy-next-door way.

Maybe Molly had a point about missing what was right in front of you. Still, it was far too late now for what-ifs and what-might-have-beens. I could only look to the future now.

Clutching a huge bouquet of flowers, a bottle of champagne,

a bronze sculpture of a gundog which was one of Browns' best-selling gifts and which I'd long admired, and a generous amount of gift vouchers, I walked out of the doors of Browns for the last time.

It was the end of an era and the start of a brand new one.

Thankfully I had no time to sit and contemplate my last day at work and whether or not I'd done the right thing in leaving. No sooner had I got home than I'd changed out of my old work clothes and deposited my company sweatshirt in the bin. After showering I put on my black shift dress, some strappy heels and a silver pendant, and tied up my hair casually on top of my head.

I was hoping for a not trying too hard, simple but effective look, and judging by Alex's open-mouthed expression when I opened the door, I was pretty certain I'd pulled it off.

'You look... incredible.' Alex savoured every syllable in the word, his obvious admiration making my legs unsteady on my heels and turning my insides to mush. 'I brought you flowers,' he said, handing over the biggest bouquet I'd ever seen.

If I'd thought my flowers from work were beautiful then this profusion of blooms including oriental lilies and large pink headed roses was in a different league altogether.

'Wow. Thank you,' I said, lowering my nose to inhale their delicious scent. I leant up to kiss him on the cheek, catching a whiff of another more masculine scent, which was even more seductive. 'That's so lovely of you.'

'It's my pleasure,' he smiled.

I'd been with my ex for nine years and I don't think he'd ever bought me so much as a single red rose so this pleasure was definitely all mine, especially as Alex's mouth was curling in a way that made my stomach react in the same way.

'Well, it's not every day you leave your job, is it? How was your last day at work?'

'Emotional, I think that's the best way to describe it. I always hate goodbyes and today there were plenty of them. There were lots of laughs and lots of tears too. Must admit I'm feeling a bit wrung out now.'

'What you need is a pick me up. Come on, madam,' he said, holding up his arm for me. 'Your carriage awaits.'

We ended up in a French restaurant that was tucked away in an alley leading down to the river. It was intimate and welcoming and reassuringly the conversation, aided by the wine, flowed effortlessly, just as it had when we'd first met at the wedding.

'So what made you decide to leave your job now?' Alex asked me between courses. 'You'd been there quite some time, hadn't you?'

'Ever since I left school. It's the only job I've ever known and I think that was part of the problem. I realised I'd been standing still for far too long, ever since my mum died actually. My life stopped then and it never really started again, not properly. At twenty it seemed like I had all the time in the world, but with my thirtieth looming in a couple of years, I just feel this desperate need to do something with my life, to try something new, something adventurous, so that I don't feel life is passing me by.'

'Really?' said Alex, amusement flickering over his features. 'Like what?'

'Well, quitting my job was the first step. I want to devote more time to all the projects I've wanted to do for so long now like writing and crafting, and generally living life to the full. I want to feel as though I'm taking part in life instead of watching it happen to other people from the sidelines. Can you understand that, Alex?'

'Yes, absolutely.' He nodded, his gaze doing that unnerving thing of travelling around my face, seeming to examine each and every pore and freckle, before landing with a heavy thump on my eyes. I felt my lashes give an involuntary flutter. 'Well, if it's an adventure you're looking for I'm sure I can help you out. If you want me to.'

His eyes flickered at me and I dropped my gaze, away from his intense scrutiny. I couldn't admit to Alex that even being with him here tonight was an adventure in itself.

'I'm sure you could, Alex,' I said, my head ignoring the suggestive edge to his words, but my body responding in its own sweet way. I felt the temperature inside my veins soar, sending my heart racing. 'It sounds to me as though you live a pretty full and exciting life as it is. Working in the city, then setting up your own gallery, painting, travelling the world. You've crammed in so much more than me.'

'Well, we all travel different paths in life. It's no good comparing yourself to other people and what they've done. You have to live your own life, do what's right for you, but it's never too late to take a change of direction.'

'Yes, well, that's what I'm doing now. It feels like the right time. I don't know what the future will hold for me, but I'm feeling really excited about the prospect.'

'See, what did I tell you? You didn't believe me when I told you I could see big changes in your future, but already my predictions are taking shape.'

He raised his eyebrows at me as a delicious smile lifted one corner of his mouth.

'Oh, your famous letter,' I said, laughing. 'If you'd let me read it then I might agree, but I wasn't even allowed to see it. You could have written any old nonsense in that letter. In fact, I know you probably did.'

His brow furrowed as he chewed on his lips, looking at me doubtfully.

'You're doubting my insight again, Jen. You shouldn't. Believe me, I know what I'm talking about, and who knows, you might even get to find out what was in that letter one day. Your problem is you're far too impatient. It will happen for you, I promise. Everything you want and desire is out there waiting. You just need to reach out and grab for it.'

The way he said it, with such conviction and sincerity, could make me believe he knew exactly what he was talking about, but I shook my head, indulgently. It didn't matter that Alex was humouring me. He had about as much insight into my future as I had into the foreign stock exchange, but his advice was spot on, resonating with me deep down inside. It was the same advice my mum left for me in her letter; to get out there and live my life to the full. Advice I was ready to take now.

I rolled my shoulders and wriggled back into my chair, allowing a sense of wearied contentment to wash over me. It had been a week of highs and lows, my emotions laid bare, but I couldn't think of a better way to round it off than to spend it here with Alex.

'You know, Jen, I'm really pleased you came tonight,' he said, as if picking up on my thoughts. Maybe there was something to his claims about second sight, after all. His hand reached out for mine across the table and our eyes met, his touch sending a jolt of electricity reverberating down my spine. 'I've been looking forward to seeing you again, ever since the last time, and for a while there I thought it might never happen. You have to give a guy points for persistence,' he said, with a wry smile.

I laughed.

'Oh, I do give you that. I really like you as well, only…'

How could I possibly explain my feelings when I could barely make sense of them myself? Alex had been incredibly persistent. Charming, flattering and attentive too. It made my head spin and my body capitulate, and yet there was still something about him that unsettled me. However hard I tried I couldn't rid myself of Angie's words of warning. Could I trust Alex not to break my heart? The way he was looking at me now, intently, peeling away the layers to my innermost desires and feelings, I suspected not.

'I get it,' he said, holding up a hand. 'It's you, not me.' He pressed his lips together, nodding in understanding. 'Really, it's fine, Jen. I don't want to put any pressure on you.'

Why was I allowing my emotions to get so muddied in what should be just a carefree, enjoyable fling with a drop-dead gorgeous man? The night I'd spent with Alex had been memorable and magical. An experience definitely worth repeating.

After dinner we walked the short distance along the path that ran alongside the river, hand in hand, our fingers entwined, before we jumped into a taxi, Alex giving my address to the driver. When the car pulled up outside my flat, Alex got out and held the door open for me.

'Would you like to come up for a coffee?'

'I can't think of anything I'd like more,' said Alex, stroking my cheek with his thumb. 'But not tonight. I've got an early start in the morning. And you,' he said, smiling, 'look absolutely whacked.' He leant down to kiss me, depositing the lingering taste of red wine into my mouth. He pulled away, tracing a finger over my lips where his mouth had just been. 'Beautiful, but whacked. You definitely need your bed.'

'Oh…' my disappointment escaped my lips. I needed my bed, it was true, but I needed Alex beside me in my bed, to feel the strength of his firm hard body against mine, to feel the exquisiteness of his kisses on my skin. I'd been reconciling myself to the idea all night long. In truth, it hadn't been a difficult decision, but now it looked as though Alex had other ideas. 'Are you absolutely certain?' I said, trying to keep the note of desperation from my voice.

He nodded resignedly.

What was going on? Could I have misread the signs? Did he have the owner of the earrings waiting for him at home?

'Okay,' I said, gathering my pride. 'Thanks for a lovely evening, Alex.'

'The pleasure has been all mine.' He kissed me again, this time gently, fleetingly, on my lips and my mouth chased his kiss as he pulled away, extricating himself from our embrace. 'I'll give you a call in the week.'

'Great. I'll look forward to it.'

Would he, wouldn't he? Should I, shouldn't I? My poor little heart; taunted, teased and tempted by its flirtation with Alex Fellows. Really, I wasn't sure how much more of this my heart or I could take.

13

The next morning I woke late and stretched out in my bed, savouring the sensation of not having to rush out of bed for anybody or anything. My mind played over the events of the last twenty-four hours and I felt a warm swell of gratitude for the love and affection shown to me from the friends and colleagues who had played such an important part in my life for so long. Spending the evening with Alex had been the perfect way to end the day, but it had only fed my desire for more of him; to discover more about the man who was becoming more interesting, enticing and equally unfathomable with every moment that I spent in his company.

Was I sweating the small stuff, as my mum would have said? Over-thinking things. Why couldn't I just go with the flow and see what happened. I'd already convinced myself there could be no long term future with a man like Alex, so why was I playing over every conversation in my head, reliving every shared look and touch, analysing every nuance between us as though there might.

'Stop it!' I chastised my reflection in the mirror. If I was going to be moving forward with my life, I needed to put Alex very firmly out of my head.

I ran the bath, pouring mango and passionfruit bubbles into the running water. I made myself a milky coffee and warmed up a *pain au chocolat* in the oven before retreating to the heavenly depths of the hot water, turning the music up loud and putting all thoughts of gorgeous distracting men out of my mind. There were plenty of other things that needed my full-on attention and on Monday I would start with a vengeance on my new life.

After climbing out of the bath I changed into some tracksuit bottoms and a sweatshirt as I was going to spend the day taking photos of the craft projects I'd recently completed. Rummaging through the drawer for my camera I gave a cursory glance to my mobile sitting on the side. Four missed calls from an unknown number.

I wandered out to the hallway and noticed the insistent flashing of the answer machine, demanding my attention. Panic fluttering in my chest, I pushed the button to hear the messages.

'Hello Jennifer, it's Marcia here. I wonder if you could give me a ring... my number is, now let me see, it's here somewhere, right... 03797 214 024.'

'Hello Jennifer, it's Marcia. I left a message, but I'm wondering if you received it. Do you think you could call me. The number is... hang on... 037...'

'Hello again, Jennifer. I've tried you on this phone and on your mobile one, but I can't seem to get hold of you. It's your granddad. I don't want you to worry, but he's had a funny turn. We're at the hospital now. They're just running a few tests. Could you phone me, love, when you get this message. The number's 037...'

'No!' I stared at the answer machine accusingly. I'd only spoken to Gramps yesterday and he'd sounded absolutely fine. I made a point of ringing him every day. Surely I would have known if there'd been something wrong.

I quickly put my trainers on, grabbed my coat and keys and raced out to the car.

It took me under fifteen minutes to get to the hospital, my mind entertaining all sorts of terrifying possibilities on the way. I was just coming out of the lift on the fourth floor when I ran straight into Marcia. My heart was racing in my chest, my hands were clammy at my sides, but I'd never been so glad to see anyone in my life.

'Marcia, how is he?'

'Oh, Jennifer love. You got my messages.' She enveloped me in a hug. I wasn't sure if it was the potency of her floral, sweet perfume or the gusto of her embrace, but I felt my eyes water. 'I thought you were cross with me and ignoring my messages.' I heard the wobble in her voice.

'Oh God no, Marcia,' I said, feeling like a proper cow. 'No, not at all. I've only just picked them up, Marcia. I'm so sorry,' I took a step backwards, holding onto her arms, seeing the concern in her eyes. 'What happened? How is he?'

'He's okay, I think. He got up in the night to go to the loo and had a fall. He's got a nasty cut on the side of his head which they've stitched up. They think he's probably had a mini-stroke.'

'Oh shit! Can I see him? Where is he?'

'Just in that ward through there, love,' she said, pointing to the corridor on the left. 'I was just on my way to get a coffee. I'll fetch you one too.'

I wandered into the ward, fear in the pit of my stomach, not knowing what might be awaiting me, and saw Gramps lying in the first cubicle by the nurses' station looking every one of his seventy-eight years. I rushed to his side.

'Gramps, what have you done? I leave you alone for a day and look what happens to you.'

He stirred in his bed, his eyes fluttering open to greet me and when he smiled, tentatively, I felt a huge surge of relief. In his hospital gown he looked fragile and vulnerable, but I was simply overjoyed he was still here looking at me with love in his eyes.

'I'm fine, sweetheart. Now, I don't want you worrying.' He patted me on the hand. 'I'll be out of here before you know it, just you wait and see.'

'I do worry. You know that. And you're not going anywhere, not for a little while at least. How did it happen, Gramps?'

'I got up in the night to go for a pee and I must have taken a tumble on the way back. Don't really remember much about it. Only that I couldn't get back up again. It was Marcia who found me in the morning.'

'Oh no, you didn't spend all night on the floor, did you?'

'It's all right, love. I'm okay now.'

'Yes.' I took hold of his hand and interlocked my fingers with his, squeezing them tight. Thank goodness for Marcia. If it hadn't been for her, coming round and finding him when she did, then who knew how long he might have been stuck there. 'What have the doctors said?'

'They've done some scans. They think I've had a little stroke, that's all. They'll be doing some more tests and I'll be sent to the stroke clinic to get my medication sorted, but I'll be all right. They'll keep me in for a couple of days, I should imagine. But don't you look so worried,' he smiled. 'It could have been a lot worse.'

At the moment it hardly seemed possible. I felt dreadful that I hadn't been there for Gramps when he'd needed me and that Marcia had been trying all that time to contact me without any luck. What if it had been worse? If it had been a major stroke instead of a mini one? If Gramps' last memory of me was me storming out of his house after being rude to his friend...

'Here you are, Jen.' Marcia was back, looking the epitome of calm and level-headedness. I felt a huge wave of gratitude for her, for being there when I wasn't and for bringing an air of cheerfulness and normality to Gramps' bedside. On my own, I'd have been a quivering emotional wreck.

'Thanks, Marcia,' I said, taking the paper cup gratefully, my hands shaking. She sat down beside me and patted her hand fondly on Gramps' leg beneath the sheet.

'How are you feeling now, love?'

'Oh, you know, all right. My head's a bit sore,' he said, putting a hand up to his temple and wincing as he did so. 'I'll feel a whole lot better when I get out of this place.'

'There's no hurry, Gramps. You want to make sure they get you properly fixed up before you get home again.'

'What about Harvey? He'll be getting anxious without me. He's such a sensitive little boy.'

'Don't worry about Harvey. He can come and stay with me for a couple of days. He's used to my place and I'll be working from home now anyway so we can keep each other company.'

Gramps was the only family I had left. After losing Mum and Nan in such quick succession, I certainly wasn't ready to lose Gramps too. Who knew how long we would still have together. I didn't want to spend that time squabbling over things that really didn't matter.

'You're not to worry about anything, Harry,' said Marcia. 'We'll take care of things at home, won't we, Jen? All you need to concentrate on is getting better.'

Marcia wasn't kidding when she said she'd take care of things. In the days following Gramps' stroke, she stripped all the beds, washed every bit of linen in the house, dusted and vacuumed from top to bottom and blitzed the bathroom and kitchen with a vigour that put my lacklustre domestic skills to shame. I could have sworn she had twice as much energy and stamina as me despite being forty years older.

I worked outside in the garden, mowing the lawn and strimming the edges with Harvey mooching around behind me. All my plans were put on hold until I knew Gramps would be ready to come home from hospital. I spent one morning working out in the sunshine weeding his flowerbeds. When I was finished I went indoors and found Marcia cleaning out the oven. I flicked the switch on the kettle and pulled out two mugs from the cupboard.

'Gramps won't recognise this place when he gets home. I don't think I've ever seen the place looking so clean. Thanks for everything you've done, Marcia.'

'Well, it doesn't take long once you get started, does it?'

'Look,' I said handing her a mug of tea. 'I just want to apologise.'

'What on earth for?'

'You know, the other night when I came round. Talking to you like that, it was very rude of me.'

She smiled, and shook her head. 'It really doesn't matter. I've forgotten all about it. We've got more important things to worry about now, haven't we?'

'I know.' I sighed, feeling an unexpected surge of affection for Marcia. I'm not sure how I would have coped without her these last few days. 'Gramps' illness has made me realise just how selfish I've been. All I want is for him to be happy and healthy again.'

'Isn't that what we both want, Jen?'

'It wasn't anything against you personally, I suppose it just felt odd to have to share Gramps with someone else. It's always just been the two of us. It felt strange to see him moving on; making plans and enjoying life again. Without me. Does that sound really bad?'

'No, not at all. I understand and I would never want to come between you and your granddad. I know what a special bond you have and how much he loves you. It was one of the things I liked about him when I met him. The way he spoke about you with such obvious pride and affection. You do know you'll always come first as far as he's concerned.'

'Oh, Marcia, I'm so pleased he's got you as a friend,' I said, wondering why I'd ever felt threatened by her presence. 'Can I gave you a hug?' I asked.

She nodded, a big warm smile lighting up her face.

'It would be nice if we could be friends too.'

'Yes, I'd like that, Marcia. I'd like that very much indeed.'

14

'Could I speak to Jennifer Faraday please?'

'Yes, that's me. Here,' I said, trying to juggle six jars of chilli jam onto my dressing table, with the phone wedged into the crook of my neck. After several false starts, involving a lorry load of chillies, a ton of sugar and one not-to-be-salvaged saucepan, I'd finally managed to produce the perfect batch of chilli jam. In jars with pretty pink gingham lids, chequered labels and ribbons around the rim, I had to admit I felt pretty proud of my handiwork. Although if I intended to make my fortune selling my range of homemade products, I would seriously need to up my output and soon.

'Jennifer, it's Polly Powers from AS Recruitment. I just wondered if you were available for work at the moment?'

Blimey, I'd never expected to hear from Ms Powers after that disastrous interview and typing test a couple of months ago.

'Oh hello, Polly. Yes, yes, I am.'

'It's only a two-day assignment starting today. We had someone lined up for this job, but they've let us down at the last moment. Would you be interested?'

Last week had been a write-off with Gramps in hospital, but now he was back at home with his new medication and with Marcia keeping a close eye on him, I'd made a start on the few freelance projects I had on the go, but nothing that wouldn't keep for a little while longer. Some temporary work would fit perfectly into my new schedule. I was determined to take every opportunity offered to me.

'Yes, definitely. What is it?'

'It's a retail promotion for one of the big department stores in town. They're launching a new product and want someone to help with handing out leaflets, that kind of thing. You would need to get down there in the next hour if you are interested.'

It didn't sound very taxing, but it didn't matter. It was only for two days and until I started bringing in some regular money from my self-employed work I would have to supplement my income with anything that came my way.

While Polly gave me the details of the company, the hourly rate and what to do with my time sheets, I slipped off my dressing gown and threw it on the bed. Thankfully I'd showered so it was just a case of popping some clothes on. I could be there in less than half an hour.

First though, I just wanted to take a few quick photos of my chilli jam. I'd attempted to have a go last night, but the light had been all wrong in the kitchen. After putting the phone down on Polly, I quickly arranged the jars on my bedroom windowsill, lining them up in a row, my cream linen curtains providing a perfect frame for the shot. I snapped away happily. Today was turning into one of those perfectly productive days.

* * *

'Ah, you're here? Brilliant!'

The department manager welcomed me eagerly. Perhaps a bit too eagerly, I had cause to consider later.

'Come through. Did the agency explain what you would be doing?'

'Not really. Only that it was a promotional role.'

'Exactly. You'll be working alongside our product demonstrator who will be showing off the features of a new multi-variable vegetable slicer that is being launched today. These are very popular items at the moment, what with the interest in healthy eating, so we're expecting a big take-up. What we'd like you to do is hand out some product leaflets and discount vouchers.'

'I think I can manage that,' I said enthusiastically.

'Great. If you come out into the back, you can change into your outfit.'

'Um...' I trailed behind the manager wondering what my outfit might be. Probably a t-shirt with the company logo on. Or a baseball cap. Or a coloured sash worn over my own clothes. All of those possibilities would have been preferable to what I was actually faced with.

'A tomato?' My jaw dropped open unflatteringly. Not half as unflattering as the garish red costume being held up in front of me. 'You want me to dress up as a tomato?'

'Yes, it's fun and eye catching. You certainly won't be missed in this, will you? Would you like me to help you get changed.'

'No, I wouldn't, thank you.'

Now was the time to turn on my tail and walk straight out of here, never to come back again. As I later learned, the previous candidate for the job had done. Trouble was, if I did, I knew that Ms Powers would never forgive me and certainly wouldn't offer me any further assignments. I had a sneaking suspicion I might need Ms Powers more than she needed me at the moment. I just needed to grit my teeth and get on with it and hope these next couple of days would be over as quickly as possible.

'I can manage perfectly well on my own,' I said, with a forced smile, taking the outfit from her.

In the changing room, I pulled on some red tights, wriggled my body into the red velour bulbous costume, performing numerous contortions to hoik up the zip at the back, and stuck the green stalk hat onto my head. I observed my reflection in the mirror and grimaced. It certainly did the trick. I was miraculously, marvellously transformed into a tomato. An unhappy tomato. I took a deep breath and pulled back the curtain to the dressing room to a waiting audience which seemed to have doubled in size since I'd walked in there looking like a relatively normal human being.

'Oh, look at you,' said the manager, clapping her hands excitedly. 'You look fantastic.'

'Like a tomato,' said a bored young man to the side of her.

The rest of her entourage giggled, affection or pity shining in their eyes, I couldn't quite make out which, although I suspected they were all obviously hugely relieved that they hadn't been the ones to be roped into this particular little gem of a job.

'Come along then,' she said, handing me a wad of leaflets, 'let's get you started.'

Apart from the obvious shame and embarrassment at being cast in the role, I quickly discovered there were a number of pitfalls to being a tomato. Firstly, the material of my costume was so scratchy it brought me out in a rash. Secondly, it was so hot in there that my face quickly took on the colour of the rest of my body – pulsating a lovely shade of scarlet. Thirdly, the cut of my suit made it impossible to walk straight, instead forcing my feet out sideways, giving me an ungainly waddle. Otherwise, I think I did a pretty good job of being a tomato.

Most people gave me a sympathetic smile as they took one of my leaflets, clearly feeling sorry for me and my predicament, and children reacted in one of two ways. Either screaming in horror as the red blob with the silly grin approached them or bringing out the devil in them as they decided I could be their own personal plaything, taking it upon themselves to kick me in the shins, prod at my bulbous middle or calling me names that would make a tomato blush.

Still, I kept reassuring myself that it was only for two days and then I would never have to wear the silly costume again. Next time I'd be a bit more cautious if Polly Powers offered me a job. There would be no more dressing up as vegetables or fruit in my future that was for sure.

On the afternoon of the second day of what was turning out to be the longest assignment in history, I was just wandering around the department trying to offload my leaflets onto any unsuspecting customers when my attention drifted over to the escalator. From the top of the steps Alex Fellows emerged, looking breathtakingly handsome, like a god delivered from high up above to the kitchen department. With his tall and broad physique, highly defined features and dark wavy hair, he would command attention anywhere, but in the humdrum surroundings of a shop floor, his good looks only seemed to be accentuated.

When I saw he was heading over my way, I gulped and quickly turned away, my cheeks flushing a deeper shade of red, if that were possible. I bent down to tie my shoelaces, only realising once I got down there that I didn't actually have any shoelaces. I held out my hand to the floor to steady a threatening wobble, but because I was so top heavy it was a futile gesture. I had no chance of stopping myself as I toppled over in an ungainly heap –

landing on my back, legs akimbo, straight into the path of Alex Fellows.

'Goodness,' he said, almost falling on top of me, 'are you all right?'

He bent down to look at me, but I turned my face into my collar, hoping he wouldn't recognise me beneath the tomatoey disguise. I attempted to roll over, but I couldn't get enough momentum and only ended back where I started, my legs swinging wildly in the air.

'Here,' he said, and I felt sure I recognised a warm note of humour in his voice. 'Let me help you up?'

With Alex's assistance, I clambered to my feet, tucking my chin into my neck and dropping my head to my chest, a very shy tomato now, wondering if I could scoot away without being spotted, but it was no good, Alex was far too perceptive for that.

'Hey, Jen, that's not you under there is it?' He tipped my chin up with his finger and I lifted my head to look into his eyes. Warm bluey/brown/grey eyes that were smiling at me now, matching the big grin spreading across his face. 'It is you. Well... this is a surprise. Fancy that.' He fell silent for a moment, his gaze travelling up and down the length of my body. His eyebrows rose as he chewed on the inside of his lip. He was trying desperately not to laugh, I could tell. 'What are you doing here? And, I suppose an obvious question, but why are you dressed as a tomato? Is this a new career for you now?'

I squirmed in my suit. I couldn't have turned redder if I'd tried. No wonder Alex looked shocked. I'd have been equally surprised if I'd found him cavorting around somewhere disguised as a vegetable.

'It's a favour for a friend. My friend, Polly. She was a bit desperate and asked if I could help her out so I said yes. A friend in need and all that. It's only for today. Thankfully.'

'Right, I see. Well, I think I see,' he said, still smiling. 'With friends like that... eh?'

'Yes,' I forced a laugh, wishing he would go away now. Couldn't he tell my ritual humiliation was complete?

'Right, well, I should get on and leave you to whatever it is you should be doing.' He turned as if to walk away, before turning back again. 'Oh Jen, I called you, but got your voicemail again. We're on first name terms now, I've spent that long chatting to it. I didn't leave a message this time, but was wondering if you were free this Saturday.'

I swallowed hard, amazed that an extremely attractive man was asking me out while I was dressed as a tomato. Maybe my powers of attraction were much stronger than I thought.

'Yes, I think I might be,' I said, wondering why I was even attempting to appear seductive. I was never going to pull it off in this get-up.

'Good, how about we head outdoors. A day out in the countryside, would you fancy that?'

'Sounds good to me.'

'Great. I'll pick you up at nine a.m.' He paused, took a step backwards and looked me over again as if he still couldn't quite believe it was me he was talking to. 'Oh, and Jen, do you know something?'

'What?'

'You really do make a very fetching tomato.'

15

'Are you always such a nervous passenger?'

I was certain I detected a gleeful look in Alex's eye as he threw the Land Rover around yet another sharp corner and my hands clutched on tighter to the edge of the seat. Alex's gung-ho style of driving, as though he was competing for the leading position in a cross-country rally, hadn't been quite so noticeable when we were bombing up the motorway but now, navigating narrow country lanes, I felt sure my life was in imminent danger.

'No, never before,' I said, bracing my legs wide to the floor to counteract being flung from one side of the car to the other. 'This is a first for me.' I looked down briefly to see my knuckles white against the seat before fixing my gaze on the road ahead again, acting as un-appointed chief look-out for any traffic coming from the opposite direction. I was ready to scream, slam my foot down on my imaginary brake and hide my head in my hands for what I felt certain was an accident waiting to happen.

Alex chuckled as though he was pleased with my answer. I smiled weakly in return, wishing to goodness he wouldn't turn to look at me like that. 'Keep your eyes on the bloody road,' I was silently chanting.

'Don't worry, you're in safe hands. Della's never let me down yet,' he said, tapping his hands fondly onto the steering wheel. 'She can give a bit of a bumpy ride at times, but she's totally roadworthy.'

'That's reassuring to know,' I said, not wanting to mention that I was more concerned about the driver and his credentials than the vehicle.

When Alex had mentioned a day out in the country I'd imagined a leisurely visit to the seaside or a country park where we would walk for miles along unchallenging territory. I loved walking and had hoped we might round off the day with a romantic picnic on a riverbank overlooking some pretty scenery. It was only after we'd been in the car for several hours, climbing increasingly narrow roads up into the hills that I got the first inkling that this wasn't going to be any ordinary day out. My imagined scenarios were looking less and less likely by the moment.

'You still haven't told me where we're going.'

'Well, if I told you then it wouldn't be a surprise, would it?'

'Did I mention I don't like surprises? Hate them, in fact. I need to know what I'm doing or else I get terribly anxious.'

'Ah right. This could be awkward then,' said Alex, chuckling to himself. 'Look, hopefully you'll like this surprise. And if you don't, well there's not a lot I can do about it now.'

I sat back in my seat and let the unfamiliar countryside whizz by. Half an hour later we finally arrived at our destination. He parked in a huge gravel car park and we both climbed out.

'Come on,' he said, marching ahead, clearly expecting me to follow him. A feeling of trepidation was growing in my stomach with each passing moment as I realised that Alex's and my own definition of fun might differ greatly. Everywhere I looked there was a warning sign of sorts, although I was still struggling to work out what we might actually be doing. Anything that involved safety gear, warning notices showing falling rocks, and the great outdoors didn't sound like a lot of fun to me.

'I thought you said you wanted an adventure. This is it, Jen.' Alex flexed his arms out to the side taking a big deep breath. 'Today's the day. Don't worry though, I think you're going to love it.'

I wasn't so sure about that.

'No, I might give it a miss. Whatever it is. I'll watch from the sidelines and cheer you on. I'm happy to do that. I've always been a good spectator.'

'Nope, sorry Jen. I'm afraid that's not an option.'

He took me into a large log cabin where a couple of hearty types looked me up and down and assessed my body shape, which was most disconcerting. Ten minutes later I was dressed in a bright yellow jumpsuit, had a black harness wrapped unflatteringly around my nether regions, a tin hat on my head and a huge surge of adrenalin racing around my veins.

When we got back outside Alex bent his head down to avoid the contraption fixed to my head and peered into my eyes.

'Are you all right?'

'Do I look all right? No, I'm not all right. I look absolutely ridiculous in this get-up and feel sick to my stomach.'

In fairness I probably didn't look any more ridiculous than I had a few days earlier when I'd bumped into Alex in the department store dressed as a tomato, but at least then I was only required to look the part. Here, I suspected something else might be required of me.

I looked and felt totally self-conscious, whereas Alex managed to look quintessentially cool, rugged and totally at ease in his gear. As though he should be appearing on the cover of Outdoor Pursuits Monthly. A big smile spread across his lips.

'Come on, Jen, shall we go and get this done?'

'Do we have to? Can't we please just go home? Find a nice little pub where we can warm ourselves up and get something to eat?'

'Ha ha, you're so funny, Jen. Of course we can't go home, we've only just got here. Don't worry, you'll love it. I promise you will. Come over here, let me show you.'

He took hold of my hand and led me over to a viewing platform. From our vantage position high up in the sky, sheer cliffs descended to either side of us lining a vast lake that disappeared off into the distance. It looked as though we were on the edge of the world and I was desperate to get off.

'What happens? How do we get down?' I asked, not really wanting to know the answer. 'Is there some sort of cable car,' I said, suddenly spotting the parallel wires running from another platform a little further along. A cable car would be okay. I could close my eyes and hang onto Alex's arm for dear life.

'It's a zip wire. You'll be harnessed to that overhead cable and travel down the line over the water. It's the most amazing experience, Jen. Exhilarating.'

'Ha ha ha ha ha ha,' I laughed in a breathless, slightly hysterical fashion so that the people gathered on the other platform looked over at me. I looked at Alex who was wearing his absolutely deadly serious face. 'What? You're not kidding? You really expect me to risk my life by going on that thing? No way!'

'You'll be fine. It's perfectly safe. And we'll go down at the same time. You did say you wanted a bit of excitement and adventure, Jen. What better place to start.'

I gulped. Alex clearly knew nothing about me. If he did he would know that this was wrong on so many levels. When I'd said adventure I meant purely from an observational standpoint, not from a gung-ho, let's get involved standpoint. I'd wanted to travel and see wonderful sights around the world; I wanted to stand on a remote golden beach and gaze in awe at a magnificent night sky; I wanted to explore clear blue Caribbean seas and its collection of exotic marine life from the safety of a glass-bottomed boat or view powerful raging waterfalls against a backdrop of dramatic scenery.

If none of those things were available I'd be more than happy to be wined and dined by an extremely gorgeous man and then spend the night with him in his bed while he made mad passionate love to me. My views on casual relationships had changed dramatically over the last couple of weeks, especially as far as Alex was concerned.

One thing I knew for certain was that I didn't want to be freezing my tits off on what was turning out to be the coldest day of the year, standing on the edge of a cliff, being coerced into what was a certain step to my imminent death.

'Alex, I'm sorry, this is really lovely of you to arrange this, but I simply can't do this. I don't do heights, I'm afraid.'

He grabbed hold of my forearms and looked into my face, his eyes beseeching.

'You can do this, Jen. It is the most wonderful life-affirming experience. When you take a step off that platform and whizz down that line it will take your breath away. You will never have felt so alive in your whole life. You'll get to the other side and have the most amazing feeling of joy and satisfaction.'

'The other side? I'm really not ready to go there, Alex.'

'Stop it,' he said. I could tell he was trying not to laugh and at that moment I thought my infatuation with Alex might be well and truly over. Yep, there were definitely more fish in the sea. Preferably more of the friendly laidback variety than the woman-eating shark variety. His grasp, on my shoulders now, tightened.

'You're shaking. I promise you I wouldn't have brought you here if I didn't think you could do this. I promise you, you'll thank me for this when you're standing at the other side feeling a wonderful sense of accomplishment.'

'I'll thank you when you've got me home, safely in one piece,' I grumbled.

I could feel my teeth chattering and my whole body trembling with fear and cold.

'See that kid over there. He's twelve and he's been down three times already. If he can do it, you can too, Jen.'

'Bully for him!' I said petulantly. 'He's clearly that type of irritating child who does wild adventurous things. Like trampolining and tree climbing. I wasn't like that as a child and I'm certainly not like that now. He can go up and down a hundred times for all I care, but I don't want to!'

I could quite easily have sobbed, but I was determined to hang onto the tiny bit of dignity I had left.

'Why don't I drive down to the bottom and wait for you in the café. I'll order us a nice pot of tea and some rock cakes. Who knows, I might even live really dangerously and order some carrot cake as well. Does that sound adventurous enough for you?'

Alex wasn't impressed by my feeble attempt at humour.

'I can't force you to do this, Jen, but I think you should at least give it a try. You'll feel amazing when you've done it. I promise you. And just think how proud you'll feel. Hell, I'll be proud too. Sometimes you just need to feel the fear and do it anyway.'

This was just what I needed, a motivational pep talk from Alex. Uncharitably I gave a fleeting thought to the owner of those damned earrings and wondered what she might do in these circumstances. I felt certain she would be the adventurous type who would be only too willing to throw herself off a cliff or at Alex's feet, whatever he asked her to do.

He led me gently by the hand over to the aptly named launch platform.

'It will all be over in a few minutes,' he said ominously, as though leading me to my death – and I still wasn't sure if that was the case or not.

I closed my eyes and let myself be manhandled by the instructors who strapped me up, checked my harnesses, touched me in places no self-respecting woman wants to be touched in broad daylight, gave me a good talking to, which I think amounted to 'hold on tight' but I couldn't be entirely sure as by that stage I'd entered another realm. My eyes were stinging, my legs were wobbly and a trussed up Alex was waving at me like a lunatic from the other wire.

'We're in this together, Jen. Deep breaths and we'll go on three.' Suddenly there was a whole chorus in my ear. One... Two... On 'three', my breath was taken from me and I stepped into the abyss, a huge cavern of nothingness opening up beneath my legs.

'Oh my... aargh!' My mouth opened involuntarily and I screamed, unable to stop, although I couldn't hear any sound coming out, just the wind rushing past my ears and my suit whipping madly around my body. I dared to look down for a moment, quickly deciding that was a very bad move and focused my gaze into the distance instead.

'Aargggh!' An invisible force pressed down hard on my newly acquired accelerator button as the line picked up supersonic speed and I whizzed through the air, an unhappy uptight wasp flying on a death mission. I snapped my eyes shut and held my breath tight. When I forced myself to open them again I gasped, energised by the adrenalin rushing through my veins. An all encompassing power filled my body. Suddenly I felt super-human, invincible and totally alive, invigorated by my own bravery and the beauty of my surroundings. I was flying like a magnificent bird of prey, completely exhilarated. It was the long-est, and shortest, forty-five seconds of my life and I loved every single moment of it. As I came down to land, swooping through the air like superwoman, I realised my mouth was still wide open and now I could hear the sound belting out from my lungs. It wasn't a scream any more, but a joyous whoop of delight.

Moments later Alex ran over to greet me, a huge smile spread across his face, before he scooped me up in his arms, holding me aloft like a trophy.

'What did I tell you? You're amazing, Jen. You did it. See, you are adventurous. I knew it all along, it just needed coaxing out of you. You realise you can do anything you want to now. Doesn't that make you feel amazing?'

'Yes!'

I was bold. I was brave. I was all those things and more.

'You want to do it again?'

My feet were fixed firmly on the ground although my legs felt completely wobbly beneath me. I'd made it to the other side, hallelujah, alive and in one piece. I could do anything I wanted to. Alex was looking at me expectantly, waiting for an answer.

'Absolutely not. It was amazing, thrilling, exhilarating, but now I've found my adventurous gene, I'm putting it firmly back in its box. When it comes to adventure you can definitely have too much of a good thing!'

16

'Do you know, Jen, you surprised me today. For a moment there I honestly thought you would back out and refuse to do it.'

After our afternoon tea with clotted cream scones, which to my way of thinking was the absolute highlight of our trip, we started on the long drive home. Thankfully Alex decided to take the return journey at a much more leisurely pace and I felt much more inclined to sit back in my seat, look out of the window and watch the world go by, and truly relax for the first time that day.

'Excuse me! If I remember correctly, I did refuse to do it, but you completely ignored me,' I said, accusingly. 'You made me do it!'

He chuckled. 'I didn't make you do it. I just persuaded you that it might be a good idea and you finally came round to my way of thinking. Most people do in the end.'

'You virtually pushed me off the edge,' I said, looking across at him with half a smile.

'But can you imagine how you would feel right now if you hadn't done it? You must have an enormous sense of achievement.'

'I guess so,' I admitted reluctantly. 'But that's not to say I'd want to do anything like that ever again.'

'Some people would have walked away from that today, but you didn't. Mind you, I guess anyone brave enough to sport a tomato outfit and parade themselves in public has to be brave enough to go down a zip wire.'

If he hadn't been driving, I would have thrown something at him.

'Oh God, would you stop it.' I buried my head in my hands, my face burning red at the memory. 'I really don't want to be reminded of that day. It was awful. And then bumping into you like that. It couldn't have been more humiliating.'

'I think you fell at my feet actually, but you know, that's perfectly understandable. A lot of women do. Tomatoes too, it seems.'

I gave him a withering look. Observing him in profile as he drove, it was easy to see why women would throw themselves at him. His jawline was strong and his shoulders broad, his powerful physicality filling the car. Dark brown wavy hair framed his face. His mouth, wide and full, curled at the edges giving the impression he was permanently amused and his eyes with their multitude of hues, drew you in with their magnetic qualities.

'Seriously though, Jen,' he said, turning to give me the benefit of that gaze, 'I think it's great that you're making these changes in your life. You said you wanted to do it and now you're doing it. It must be a good feeling.'

'It is, I'm feeling confident about the future, now that Gramps is home from hospital. I'm excited to get started on all my different plans. I know there will be a lot of trial and error involved, but I'm eager to get stuck in.'

Finally I felt a sense of control over my life, steering it in a new direction of my own making. I'd spent far too long standing still. All I needed was a small push, not unlike the one Alex had given me up on that hillside today.

I'd received several small pushes in recent months, from all different directions: Angie getting married; Gramps moving on with Marcia; re-reading Mum's letter after all these years; and even Alex coming into my life had ignited my desire to grab hold of every opportunity that came my way and do something with it. I was trying not to over-think things or look too far ahead. Despite what Alex might say, no one could know what the future might hold.

'Do you fancy a nightcap?' Alex asked when we'd arrived back in Casterton.

'I'd love one,' I said. I'd been wanting a drink ever since I'd landed with a bump after my inaugural and final trip down that cable line. I think I deserved one after I'd escaped the clutches of death. And if it meant spending more time with Alex then it was all to the good.

We went to the Rose and Crown, a popular pub in town which was heaving with the Saturday night crowd. We managed to find a couple of stools at the very end of the bar. My body was aching with tiredness but my mood was heady and light.

'Here's to new beginnings,' said Alex, raising his glass to mine.

'New beginnings,' I said, feeling a flutter of excitement in my stomach.

'You know, if there's anything you think I might be able to help with then you only need to ask. Obviously I don't know anything about your particular line of work, but I do have quite a few contacts locally I can put you in touch with if you're interested; there's a great accountant I use and the editor of the local newspaper is a friend of mine, so I can always put a good word in for you if you wanted to pitch him some ideas.'

'Thanks, Alex,' I said, touched by his offer. He was looking at me with a genuine warmth and sincerity in his eyes. He'd seen me at my best, on the day of Angie's wedding, and at my worst, when I was dressed as a tomato, and he seemed to like me in both guises, treating me with kindness and respect. Before he'd picked me up this morning I wondered if there might be any awkwardness between us or if we would run out of things to say to each other, but twelve hours later and the excitement and anticipation I felt was as if I was seeing him for the first time again.

'I've really enjoyed myself today, Alex, and I've done something that I wouldn't have done if it hadn't been for you.'

'Well, I'm really glad you came. It's been great. Definitely worth the wait,' he said, giving me a barely perceptible wink that spoke straight to my insides. His hand reached out for mine on my lap and our eyes met, his touch sending a jolt of electricity reverberating down my spine. He moved his stool closer to mine so that our knees were touching, his hand slipped onto my waist and it was as if all the noise and hubbub of the bar drifted away into the background and it was only me and Alex alone in the bar. My body went into free fall as his lips landed on mine and my mouth opened involuntarily, ready to taste the sweetness of his kisses on my tongue.

I was loving more, laughing more, and I hadn't given a second thought to the cream scones, cucumber sandwiches and fruit cake I'd polished off with gusto this afternoon. Mum would definitely have approved. What did it matter if it was only for the moment? Here was exactly where I wanted to be right now.

The nicely romantic intimate mood we'd created was shattered by someone barging into my stool, almost sending me toppling over the side.

'Well, well, well! Look at you two getting cosy together!'

We both looked up at the same time as we felt an arm around our shoulders. Tom was standing between us, grinning broadly. He gave me a wet and sloppy kiss on the cheek and I had to resist the urge to shudder and wipe it away.

'Hi!' Alex and I said in unison, dropping our hands and giggling as though we had something to be embarrassed about, which of course we didn't. Seeing Tom swaying between us dashed my good mood immediately. Not only had he wrecked a lovely moment between Alex and me but he was clearly way ahead of us in the drinking stakes, and without his lovely wife at his side too.

'So, what's going on? Are you two an item now?' he asked, laughing, patting Alex heartily on the back.

'No,' said Alex quickly. A bit too quickly if I'd stopped to think about it, but that wasn't my major concern right now. 'We've just been catching up, that's all.'

I looked at Tom, trying to reconcile the man in front of me with the man I saw marry my best friend just a few months ago. His smooth, charming demeanour that had been very much in evidence that day was missing now. His hair was unkempt, dark shadows circled his eyes and I felt sure if I put a match up to his mouth he would have erupted into a fireball.

'How's Angie? Is she not with you?' I asked, making a show of looking over his shoulder, knowing full well she wouldn't be.

'Aw, she's fine. Getting fatter by the day.' He swept his hand in front of his stomach, imitating a bump. 'No alcohol, no sex, she's no fun at the moment.' He winked as though I might find that remotely amusing, which I didn't.

'Really?' I nodded, biting on my lip. Only a few moments earlier I'd felt happy and light-hearted, and now Tom had waltzed in and spoilt everything. I had an anger stirring deep in my stomach, something I was having trouble keeping a lid on.

'You know, Tom, I think Angie would appreciate it much more if you were at home with her rather than propping up a bar with your mates.'

'Excuse me?' he said, looking at me as though he couldn't quite believe what I said. He turned to Alex for support, but he'd taken the moment to casually look away – suddenly finding the stem of his wine glass infinitely more interesting.

'Tom, you are newly married, your lovely gorgeous wife is pregnant with your first child and I know, because I had a long heart-to-heart conversation with her the other night, that she's feeling vulnerable, exhausted and unloved right now. You shouldn't be here with us, you should be at home providing her with support and care.'

'Woah. Give a bloke a break, Jen. For your information, I've been working hard all week. Someone has to. How else will the mortgage get paid? It's not too much to ask to want to have a couple of drinks at the weekend, is it?'

'No, but it's just not the weekends, is it?' I could hear my mouth running away from me and I could do nothing to stop it. Not that I was bothered. Someone needed to tell him. 'It's every night. You're a married man now, Tom. You can't just carry on acting as if you're still a single bloke.'

'But I've always done this,' said Tom sounding defensive. 'Alex will tell you that. Angie knows the score.'

'But that's exactly my point, Tom. You always did it in the past when you were a single man, but things have changed now. You've got to start acting more responsibly. Think about Angie for once.'

Tom grimaced and looked out of the corner of his eye at Alex, who shrugged by way of reply.

'When you split up before wasn't it because of these very reasons, Tom? You going AWOL for days on end, not turning up when you were supposed to and generally messing her around. You can't treat her like that any more.'

In fairness, he was taking my onslaught on the chin, even if he was looking a bit browbeaten right now. His shoulders had slumped and he was shifting from one foot to the other, looking like an errant schoolboy. Just in case he was thinking of turning round and doing a runner I took the opportunity to press the case home.

'It's half past ten, Tom,' I said, glancing at my watch. 'You can't expect Angie to stay up until all hours just waiting for you to roll home. Have you got any idea what it must be like for her? Sitting there all night on her own. Are you going to carry on like this when the baby arrives? I really hope not because if you do, well then honestly, Tom, I don't hold out a lot of hope for your marriage.'

'Jeez, I know we've never really hit it off, Jen, but I didn't know you were quite so strong in your dislike of me. What is this, have a pop at Tom night?'

'Jen's my friend. I want the best for her. And if I see her upset or being hurt then that upsets me too. She's a great girl and she doesn't deserve to be treated badly.'

'Oh.' Tom dropped his gaze to his feet. 'The last thing I'd want to do is hurt her. I do love her, you know?'

As he looked up at me, hollow-eyed, and as if he didn't know quite what he was doing there, I could quite believe that he did.

'Well, for goodness' sake just be a bit more thoughtful and respectful. She needs you right now, Tom, can't you see that?'

He nodded. 'Yep. Thanks, Jen. Received and understood.' He gave me a friendly salute before he looked across at Alex, a tentative smile forming on his lips. 'Still, we've got time for a quick one while I'm here, haven't we?'

Alex laughed, holding up a note to the barman, and proceeded to put in an order for a round of drinks.

'Not for me,' I said, turning to Alex, feeling a sudden wave of disappointment. 'Do you know something, Angie was right, you're just as bad as he is! Thanks for a great day, but now I really need to get out of here.'

17

I stormed out of the bar, feeling ever so slightly ridiculous, and tried to hang onto a modicum of dignity as I was fully aware of a few sets of eyes turning to look at me on the way out. I wasn't really the storming out type and I wasn't entirely sure where tonight's display of feistiness had come from, but all I knew was that I needed to get out of that place, away from those two grinning idiots.

Outside, I was grateful to feel the light wind on my face and took a breath of the cool night air, trying to gather my senses. All the time it had been just Alex and me alone together we'd got on famously, but seeing him with Tom tonight brought all of Angie's warnings to mind again. Me giving Tom a dressing down had just been a huge joke to the pair of them. I noticed the exchanged glances, the rolled eyes, the sheepish grins. They were probably having a good laugh about it now over a pint of beer. Well, good luck to them. Don't they say you should listen to your gut and my gut had been telling me ever since I met Alex that I should steer well clear.

I tucked my hands into the pockets of my jacket and was

walking along by the side of the river, looking out over the water, trying to forget what had happened when I heard a voice calling from behind me.

'Jen, wait!'

I turned round to see Alex running to catch me up. He grabbed me by the shoulders and spun me around, his eyes full of dark confusion.

'What the hell was that all about?'

I batted away his hands and walked away muttering. 'Tom. He's out of order and it just makes me so angry.'

'Yeah, I got that quite clearly, but what has that got to do with me? I thought we were having a great time there. Why did you walk out on me? What have I done that's so wrong?'

'I saw you both smirking. As though it was one big joke, but it's not, Alex! It makes me cross to think that he's still behaving as though he's a single man while Angie's stuck at home feeling sorry for herself. I saw her a few nights ago and she was in a right mess. Pregnancy can be a hard time for a woman. She needs her husband at home, not down the pub drinking himself silly.'

'For your information I wasn't smirking, but I honestly don't think it's anyone's business but Angie and Tom's. She's a big girl, she can surely fight her own battles. How can you possibly know what's going on in someone else's relationship anyway? I don't doubt you're getting Angie's side of the story, but what about Tom? Aren't there two sides to every story?'

'Really, Alex, I wouldn't expect anything less of you. You're Tom's friend and you're going to back him to the hilt whatever happens. You're two of a kind. Two peas out of the same pod. I knew that from the first day I met you. Angie warned me against you and I should have taken heed of that warning. Sorry, but I should never have come out with you today in the first place.'

'Sorry?' He grabbed hold of my wrist and pulled me closer to his body, his eyes boring down onto me. Eyes that spoke a million words in their expression as they flickered into my soul. 'What exactly did Angie say about me?'

'That's not important. This isn't about you and me. It's about Tom and Angie.'

'Well, you've just made it about me. You can't come out with comments like that and then not follow them up. Tell me what she said.'

He was staring at me, unblinking, and I gulped under the intensity of his gaze – wondering what the hell had possessed me to say that. This had got way out of hand and his proximity, the scent of his aftershave wafting beneath my nostrils and his hand clutched tightly onto mine was playing havoc with my concentration. Suddenly all the fight had gone out of me and all I really wanted was for him to kiss me again, like he had back there in the pub. I could quite easily have fallen into his arms and laid my head down on his shoulder.

'Don't worry,' I said, in what I hoped was a light-hearted way. 'Nothing too damning.' I took a step backwards to put some distance between us, but I could tell Alex wasn't satisfied with my answer. He tilted his head to one side and nodded, urging me to go on.

'Well.' I took yet another step backwards and he dropped my arm. 'All she said was that you weren't really boyfriend material.'

'Really?' His expression was dark and unforgiving. 'And why is that? According to the gospel that is Angie Cooper?'

'Something about you being a serial dater and a commitment-phobe? That you don't keep a girlfriend for longer than three months before moving on...' My voice trailed away.

'That's nice.' I could tell by the set of his mouth, the flicker of a pulse in his neck and an iciness in his eyes that he thought it far from nice, but why was he taking it so badly?

'I think she was just worried that I might get hurt,' I explained, feeling guilty that I'd broken Angie's confidence for the second time this evening. I grimaced, hoping she'd understand when I told her the circumstances. 'She didn't want me going through that again and assumed that you and I were looking for different things in a relationship. That's all.'

'Really? That's all, you reckon? Why doesn't Angie concentrate on her own relationship instead of interfering in mine?'

Alex shook his head and gestured for us to walk on, joining me at my side. The wind had picked up and the temperature seemed to have dropped by several degrees in the last few minutes. Well, it was either that or else I was being buffeted by the severe cold front wafting my way from Alex's direction.

'She was only looking out for me. That's what friends do. I look out for her. She looks out for me.'

'Everything makes absolute sense now. It's why you've been avoiding my calls, isn't it? Why you were so reluctant to see me again. Didn't you think it would be worth finding out for yourself rather than just taking Angie's word for it? I mean, she hardly knows the first thing about me.'

Anger radiated from his entire body. I hadn't intended to make him feel that way, but it was just bumping into Tom like that, and thinking about Angie and what she'd been going through these last few weeks, that had brought a whole set of emotions bubbling to the surface.

'What happened to Tom?' I asked, to break the ensuing silence.

Alex shrugged, a rueful smile on his lips. 'He decided to go home. With his tail between his legs, I don't doubt.'

'I'm sorry,' I said, although I couldn't feel any remorse for what I'd said to Tom. He'd needed telling and as his wife's best friend, I was the person to tell him. Although there was a tiny part of me that worried Angie might be upset with me. I hoped she'd realise I was only trying to help. Someone needed to point out a few home truths to her husband.

'I didn't mean to spoil the evening,' I said now to Alex. 'It was a lovely day up until that point. And I apologise for having a go at you. It really wasn't about you.'

'No, I get that.' He stopped and put a hand on my shoulder, turning my body to face him. 'Look, let's not allow what happened back there to spoil what's left of the evening. Come back to mine for coffee, Jen,' he said, his hand finding my waist again, his lips, detectable kissable lips, a hair's breadth away from my own.

Alex was right. I had been pushing him away just because I was too scared to let my defences down and let him in. Angie's cautionary words had struck a chord deep within me, but I realised now that I should do as Alex had said and make my own mind up about him, not base my judgement on something Angie had told me. Still, my head was telling me to make my excuses and get myself out of there as quickly as possible – but my heart was telling me something else entirely.

His ran his hand through my hair, kissing me hard on the lips, our mouths opening together as his tongue promised a thousand delights. I pulled back, looking into eyes that were heavy with longing.

'I'd like that,' I said, leaning back into the warmth of his embrace. 'I'd like that very much indeed.'

* * *

Back at his flat, Alex made me a warming hot chocolate, put some mellow jazz music on in the background and came and sat down next to me on the sofa, stretching his long legs out in front of him. If I'd hoped he might have dropped the subject of Angie and what it was she'd told me, I was very much mistaken.

He rested his arm on the back of the sofa, his hand on my shoulder now.

'I'm disappointed that you were all too eager to believe what Angie said about me. If there was something you wanted to know, you could have just asked me.'

'It wasn't like that. Really, it was just a throw away comment. Or two,' I added with a smile. 'And it wasn't only what Angie said. I knew instinctively when we met that we were two very different people. I just couldn't imagine us being together in that way.'

I wondered why was he so bothered by Angie's comments. He didn't strike me as the sort of person who concerned himself with how other people viewed him. And it wasn't as if Angie had been saying anything too bad about him. She'd hardly been spreading vicious rumours. It was only one friend talking to another. How did we ever get talking about this in the first place?

'She said lots of lovely things about you too if that makes you feel any better.' It was a case of damage limitation now. I didn't want to cause any ill feeling between Alex, Tom and Angie, but maybe it was too late for that. Tom had probably gone straight home to Angie and told her what an interfering busybody her best friend was.

'I've a feeling there's a "but" coming,' he said, a smile forming at his lips.

I laughed. 'Only that you'd left a trail of broken hearts in your wake.'

'Really?' He shook his head. 'That's unfair and not strictly accurate either. You know, I could sue her for defamation of character.'

'Don't say anything, will you? I've a feeling, after tonight, I'm already in a whole heap of trouble with Angie as it is. Besides, I don't know what you're getting so hot under the collar about. Are you really telling me that there isn't an iota of truth in what Angie said?'

'How do you mean?' he said, turning on me, his brow furrowed.

'That you're not a ladies' man, breaking women's hearts at every turn?' I was teasing him, trying to take the heat out of our conversation, but Alex was having none of it.

'Absolutely not,' he said vehemently. There was a fire crackling behind his eyes. 'Look, I don't know what her problem is with me. I've dated a lot of women, admittedly. I'll hold my hands up to that, but I didn't realise it was a crime. I'm a single man, I can choose to do as I please. And I'm always upfront with anyone I ever meet or date. I don't make promises I have no intention of keeping. If something's not working then why stay in that situation?'

'That sounds like a very pragmatic approach to dating,' I said lightly. It sounded to me as though he was only confirming what Angie had told me; that he was a single-minded, cold-hearted player. A commitment-phobe. Someone only interested in dating and sleeping with a woman before moving on to the next best thing on the block.

'Possibly.' He examined the backs of his hands. 'But I don't think it takes that long to know whether or not you're going to hit it off with someone. And there's no point in hanging around if you know ultimately it's not going to go anywhere.'

I'd only met Alex on a few occasions but already I knew how charming and utterly, hook-line-and-sinker compelling he was. I'd known that within a nanosecond of meeting him. His chameleon like eyes, searching, questioning and subtly seductive, were enough to wobble the legs of the most level headed woman.

I wondered about all those women he'd left behind and the casual abandon of their hopes and dreams and hearts. Frankly, I could see where Angie was coming from. I didn't want to be one of the ones he left behind. I'd made myself semi-immune to his charms thanks to Angie. I'd kept her warning at the forefront of my mind and a very firm, well firm-ish, lid on my heart and emotions, even if I hadn't been quite so particular with my knickers on one occasion. If Alex was going to play any part in my life then it was going to be on a no strings attached basis. I could enjoy his company for what it was; a lovely evening with an undeniably attractive man. The problem would be knowing when to walk away, with my heart and emotions still intact.

'I guess so. Do you ever think though that some of your dates might have felt differently? That they may have wanted more from you?'

'What, like Angie, you mean?' he said, with a touch of cynicism.

'Angie? How do you mean...?'

'Nothing,' he shook his head. 'Sorry, I guess I'm just annoyed that she's not exactly been singing my praises as far as you're concerned.'

'But you and Angie? There's never been anything between the pair of you, has there?'

'No, not really.' He removed his hand from my shoulder and stretched his arms in front of him, flexing his fingers.

'Not really?' I swivelled round on the sofa to face him. 'What the hell does that mean?'

'Nothing, honestly. It was just when she and Tom were on a break from each other a while ago, there was a bit of a misunderstanding between us, that's all. I've got a feeling she's not my number one fan any more.'

I looked at him aghast, trying to make sense of what he was

telling me. Angie and I didn't have secrets from each other. Well, not really. Admittedly, I hadn't told her that I'd been out with Alex a couple of times, but that was only because I knew she wouldn't approve. And I also knew that whatever Alex and I had going on between us it was only ever likely to be a temporary thing. But surely if there had ever been anything going on between her and Alex she would have told me. We were supposed to be best friends.

'What sort of misunderstanding?'

'Basically...' His lip curled apologetically. 'Well, she made a pass at me. And I knocked her back. That was all. But I wonder if she's never really forgiven me.'

'Noooo!' I jumped back on the sofa looking at him accusingly. 'I don't believe it. She would have told me.'

He shrugged, his eyebrows lifting.

'Right, well you must believe what you like.' He gave me the benefit of his intense, soul searching gaze that cut through to the depths of my stomach. It made my insides swirl, and if I'd had any doubt that Alex was lying to me, that look told me he was telling the absolute truth.

'No, I didn't mean that,' I said, trying to regain some ground, desperate to know more. 'I'm just surprised, that's all.'

'Well, I don't think there was anything serious to it. She was probably trying to get back at Tom for all the times he'd messed her around. And I think drink could have been involved too, but that's beside the point. I would never get involved with a friend's girlfriend or ex. Some things you just don't do. Besides, Angie really isn't my type. Despite what you may think, Jen, I do have some morals.'

'Of course, I just...' This snippet of juicy gossip had completely pole-axed me. Had Angie really been looking out for me? Was she concerned about my well-being and the state of my fragile heart, as she'd insisted, or was it just that she didn't want me to have something she couldn't have for herself: Alex.

'Look...' He reached out for my hand, interlocking his fingers through mine. There was a faint smile on his lips and a look of barely concealed desire in his eyes. With his other hand, he stroked his thumb down my cheekbone and traced a trail along the length of my jaw causing butterflies to stir in my stomach. 'Why are we spending so much time talking about Angie and Tom? And dating other people? All I know is that I really like you and there's no other person in the world I would want to have here with me right now than you.'

I repeated his words in my head, savouring their ripe deliciousness. Was it a line he used on other women? Did it work for him all the time? Quite honestly, I didn't care if he meant it or not. In that moment, I knew I felt exactly the same way too.

He gave me a feather-light kiss on the lips, my body immediately responding to the promise and invitation in it. Our eyes locked together, appraising each other as though it was the first time we'd set eyes on one another. His hands ran through my hair, the tips of his fingers massaging my skull, guiding my head towards his mouth, the intent in the air heavy now with desire. His tongue prised open my lips and he kissed me again, gently at first, his mouth teasing and taunting mine, sending me into a heady spiral of abandon, until our lips were pressed firmly together, our kissing even more urgent now.

Alex pulled away from me, his face flushed, a look of concern on his features.

'Listen, Jen, I'm going to be honest with you here.'

'Uh-huh.'

He held me at arms' length, but with one hand traced a finger from the top of my head down the side of my face, across my neckline and along the curve of my body. I squirmed as my whole being responded to the lightness of his touch.

'I want to take you to bed right now and get you out of those clothes.'

'O-kay.'

'I want to lay you down on my bed and kiss your entire body from top to toe and then back again and when I'm finished with doing that, which would obviously be a long and labour intensive procedure, I would like to make love to you through the night.'

'I see.' I blinked a couple of times to deflect the intensity of his gaze.

'Now, I know we've been here before and, I don't know about you, Jen, but the memories of that night we spent together are still imprinted vividly in my memory. I want to revisit that place right here and now. How would you feel about that?'

I breathed a reply, but no sound came from my mouth.

'The thing is I want to make sure you want the same thing too.'

I nodded.

'Because I know you mentioned to me before that you weren't happy with the one-night stand aspect of that evening and how you don't do casual relationships so I want to make sure, if we are going to do this, that you are one hundred per cent happy with the arrangement. Not that it would qualify in any regard as a one-night stand now. And as for a casual relationship, well, I think I would have to put that decision fairly squarely into your hands now.'

'Yes,' I whispered, uncertain if there was even a question waiting to be answered but knowing that there was only one possible answer. 'Alex?'

'Yes.'

'Would you take me to bed now please?'

18

'So, we've got a Victoria sponge, some rock cakes and a lemon drizzle tray bake. Where would you like to start, love?' Gramps handed me a cup of tea rattling around in a saucer from the posh Wedgwood tea set which had been a wedding gift to him and Nan. It rarely got an outing these days, but Nan always used to bring it out for high days and holidays, including family birthdays when she would bake one of her special chocolate sponges oozing with buttercream filling.

I took a rock cake and popped it on a pretty floral plate. I was still a bit bemused as to what I was doing here. I'd been summoned for afternoon tea which was lovely but so totally out of the ordinary as to be slightly worrying. Gramps and I didn't do arranged meetings or at least we hadn't done before Marcia arrived on the scene. I generally popped in to see him on a daily basis and, if for some reason I didn't, he'd be on the phone to me checking I was okay. So when Gramps invited me for afternoon tea saying it would be a good opportunity to catch up I knew something must be afoot.

'This all looks wonderful,' I said, taking a delicious mouthful of cake. 'Is this your handiwork then, Gramps?'

He chuckled. 'No, we have Marcia to thank for these. I was going to get some in from that lovely bakery on Celtic Street, but Marcia insisted it would be just as easy for her to make some. She's a great cook. Not as good as your nan mind, but still very good.'

I smiled, touched by his unending loyalty to his wife.

'I did think Marcia might be here this afternoon.'

'No, of course she would have liked to come, but she's off visiting some friends. Besides, I thought it would be nice to spend some time together, just the two of us.'

'Oh Gramps, I hope you don't think you have to do this now after I made such a fuss that day when Marcia was here. I'm so sorry about that. I did apologise to Marcia. I think I must have been having a bad week.'

'I know, I know. And that was never a problem. It's all forgotten about now.'

'Well, that's good, Gramps, because I would hate to think there was any bad feeling between us. I got to know Marcia a bit better when you were in hospital and I can see what a lovely lady she is.'

'She is, indeed.'

'So, I'm delighted to be here, but are we celebrating anything in particular?'

'No. Well, only me still being here after my little stay in hospital,' he chuckled. 'That has to be something to celebrate.'

'Definitely,' I said, smiling. 'It's good to see you looking so fit and well. You gave us all quite a scare there, you know that, don't you?' I let my arm dangle down by the side of my chair to give Harvey a cuddle and a sneaky tidbit of cake. He lapped it up greedily and noisily.

'Yes, it gave me a scare too, I can tell you. And I suppose it got me thinking.'

'Oh?' I glanced across at him. I hadn't been fooled by his assertion that the tea and cakes were just an excuse for a catch-up. I knew him far too well for that. 'Come on then, spill the beans, I know there's something that you want to talk to me about.'

'Well, I suppose it's a bit delicate. One of those things you don't like to speak of.'

'You can tell me, you know that, Gramps.' I was getting concerned now, seeing his troubled expression. Had he received some bad news from the hospital? 'What is it? You're getting me worried now.'

'Oh, it's nothing to worry about. I just wanted you to know that I've been to the solicitor's and had my will properly drawn up.' I could feel the relief seep from my shoulders.

'You have?'

'Yes. I wanted to get everything in order and to know that when I go you won't have a mess of paperwork to deal with. I've got a folder here with all the details in of my will and a few insurance policies, and the solicitor's details too. I'll keep it in the top drawer of the bureau.'

'Okay, Gramps, although I really do hope you're not intending on going anywhere soon.'

He smiled, his warm brown eyes shining. 'Definitely not, but I feel happier knowing I've got my affairs in order. I can forget about it all now and get on with my life. Of course, everything will be coming to you; the house and a couple of small savings plans. It'll give you a bit of security at least for when you're older and have a family of your own.'

'Aw, Gramps.' I reached over and squeezed his hand and I had to swallow hard on the emotion forming at the back of my throat.

I didn't want to think about a time when I would need to see that wretched folder again, but I could appreciate the peace of mind it gave to Gramps knowing everything was sorted out now.

'You know,' I said, trying to inject some light-heartedness into the conversation, 'there's still time to sell the house and cash in your insurance policies and use them to fund a luxury world cruise or buy an Italian sports car or a little cottage by the sea.'

'Ha, I'll bear that in mind, but actually, love, I'm really happy with my lot here. I couldn't leave this place because it would be like leaving your nan behind. Then there's my allotment and you and Harvey. Everything I love and hold dear is around here. I don't ask for anything more than that really. And I've got Marcia to think about too now.' He dropped his gaze, wet his finger with his tongue and picked up the crumbs from his plate. 'You do like Marcia, don't you, Jen?'

'Of course, I just said so, didn't I?'

'Yes, but you're not just saying that to keep me happy, are you?'

'No, of course not. I must admit I felt a bit strange about it when you first got together, but now I think it's really lovely that you found such a good friend in her.'

'Good, good. Just thought I'd check because I've been doing a lot of thinking in that direction.'

'Have you?' I said, intrigued now.

'Yes.' He was wringing his hands together, looking more uncomfortable by the moment. 'Oh, there's no easy to way to say this, Jen, but I wanted to ask how you'd feel if Marcia and I, well if we... you know... got together... took our relationship to the next level?'

I looked at him, eyes wide, wondering what on earth it was he was asking me.

'The next level?'

'Yes. Marcia's come to mean a bit more to me than being just a friend these last few weeks.'

'Oh, I see,' I said, not really wanting to think about the implications of that.

'Being ill like that, so suddenly and unexpectedly, made me realise just how precious life can be. I don't know how long I've got left, love, but I do know I want to make the most of every moment I'm given. Your nan was the love of my life. My soulmate. And no one will ever replace her in my heart. But to be honest with you, I'm not very keen on living on my own and Marcia and I have become very good companions. I thought I might ask her to marry me?'

'Marry her?' Hastily I rearranged my features to cover up my complete shock. I felt a physical pain in my chest.

'I know I said there would be no other woman for me, after your nan went, but I've got to face facts, love, your nan's not here any more and Marcia is. And I think it would make Marcia happy to put things on a more formal footing. But I wanted to talk to you about it first because you know I would never want to do anything that might upset you.'

'You don't think it's a bit soon? Shouldn't you wait until you know each other a little better. What's the hurry?'

Gramps gave a small laugh and a disapproving look.

'Sweetheart, I'm seventy-eight! That's the hurry! It's not as though I've got a lot of time left, but what I have got I want to spend with the woman I love. What's so wrong with that?'

'Nothing, I suppose.' I'd grown fond of Marcia, yes, but I wasn't sure I fancied her as my step-grandmother and to hear him say he actually loved her pierced my heart in a way I wasn't sure I wanted to acknowledge.

'You know sometimes I've felt as though I've been holding you back, Jen. That you feel a responsibility for me that is stopping you from living your own life to the full. I don't want that. To be a burden on you. I've got Marcia now to keep an eye out for me. That's not to say that you won't always be at the centre of my world. You're the light of my life, you know that?' He leant over and tipped my chin with his finger. 'But I want you to get out there and do your own thing without having to worry about me the whole time.'

'I've never felt you've been holding me back,' I said, trying hard to hide the sadness from my voice. Everything I'd ever done for Gramps I'd only done because I'd wanted to. Maybe it was the other way around and it was me cramping his style. Is that what he was trying to tell me?

'Sorry, if I've made you feel that way,' I added.

'Don't be silly. You've nothing to apologise for. You're the best granddaughter I could ever have wished for. But if I'm going to be marrying Marcia, I would want to do that knowing I had your blessing.'

I took a deep breath, pulled up my big girl knickers and plastered a big smile on my face. 'If it's what you want then of course you have my blessing, Gramps. Come here,' I said, beckoning him over for a hug. 'I'm really happy for you.'

I buried my head in his woolly cardigan knowing that things would never be the same again. That part of our life, just me and Gramps together – playing Scrabble, going down the club for a pint of beer and a glass of wine, nights spent in watching repeats of *Midsomer Murders* – was over. Maybe it was a good thing. If I was ever going to do all those things Mum would have wanted me to I couldn't be stuck at home every night with Gramps watching telly.

'I can't tell you what a relief that is, Jen. I haven't asked Marcia yet, I wanted to clear it with you first. Honestly, if you'd said to me you didn't want me to do it, then I wouldn't go through with it. Your happiness means that much to me, Jen, you know that.'

'Oh Gramps, you've got to start putting yourself first. It'll be amazing, a new chapter in your life. I can just imagine Marcia's face when you ask her. Have you decided how you might do it?'

'Well, I won't be getting down on one knee, that's for sure. If I did that, I might never get back up again, but I'll make sure to make a special occasion of it. I'll take her out to a posh restaurant and propose over a romantic dinner. I don't know what she'll say. She might turn me down yet so I wouldn't start shopping for a new dress just at the moment. We'll have to wait and see.'

'Don't be daft. There's no way Marcia is going to say no, she's going to be so thrilled.'

First Angie and now Gramps. Didn't they say weddings, like buses, come in threes. I gave a passing thought to who might be next.

'I'm so glad we've got that out in the open because I don't like us having any secrets, do you?'

'No, of course not.'

Gramps fell quiet for a moment, looking at me gravely from across the table.

'So there's nothing you want to tell me about then?' he asked.

I shifted uneasily in my chair.

'Er no, why?'

'Well, I just had an inkling, call it a grandfather's intuition, that there might be something going on in your life that you're keeping from me. Not that I want to intrude. I'm sure if there is anything you'll tell me in your own time.'

There was a mischievous twinkle to his eye and I wondered how he could possibly know. Was it because I'd been going round with a silly smile on my face these last few days or had he noticed a glow to my skin that had been missing in recent months?

I never could keep anything from him.

'Oh Gramps,' I said, giving him a shy smile. 'How could you tell? There is someone but it's early days yet. We've been out a couple of times together, but I honestly don't know if it will go any further than that. He's different to any man I've met before. He's intelligent, funny, rich, oh and drop-dead handsome too.' I could hear the note of longing in my own voice. 'I really like him, but I'm not certain how he feels about me or if he's ideal boyfriend material.'

'Ha ha, is that so,' said Gramps, a smile lighting up his face. 'Well, I wasn't expecting that!'

'You weren't? But you said...'

'No, this is what I meant,' he said, getting out the local paper from the wicker basket and opening up the pages. Pride of position on page three was a glorious colour photo of a lovely lady showing off the delights of a vegetable slicer standing next to a plump ripe tomato on legs.

'Oh my god!'

'It is you, isn't it? I knew it! I'd recognise that cheeky smile and those shapely calves anywhere. What on earth were you doing, love?'

I giggled. 'It was a job. Thankfully only a two-day job, but yes, I took the starring role of the tomato. I'm only pleased they didn't publish my name in that article. Only a granddad would recognise me beneath that outfit. I'm sure no one else would.'

'Yes, I think you're probably right.' Gramps was still laughing. 'The lads down at the Legion couldn't believe it was you when I showed them.'

'Please tell me you didn't, Gramps?'

He nodded affectionately. 'Well, I'm proud of you whatever

you do. Look, you'll have to bring your new young man round here so I can get to meet him. I'll give him the once-over and tell you whether I think he's right for you. Mind you, I remember you thinking the last one was ideal boyfriend material and look what happened to him!'

'Yeah, you're right there, Gramps,' I said with a sigh.

Gramps tilted his head to the ceiling, a mischievous smile on his lips.

'What do you think your nan would be saying if she's up there looking down at us right now?'

'Ooh, she'd be furious about you getting married again, I'm sure!'

'I know, she'd be bloomin' livid.' His laughter was so contagious that I couldn't help myself from joining in. 'She'd be loving you as a tomato though. That would keep her giggling for days on end. And as for that new young man of yours, I'm sure your nan will be putting him through an extensive vetting procedure as we speak. If she thinks he's right for you, then everything will work out for the best and if she doesn't, it won't. It's as simple as that.'

If only it was as simple as that, I thought with a wry smile.

'Life has to move on, isn't that right, Jen? For all of us. You know, in the absence of some champagne, do you think we ought to have another pot of tea and an extra slice of cake to celebrate this fantastic news?'

Any excuse for an extra slice of cake was always a good one for me. While Gramps refilled the teapot I cut into the lemon drizzle cake. I'd be delighted to extend my congratulations to Marcia the next time I saw her. Anyone who could make cakes as good as these had to be a welcome addition to our little family.

19

I'd spent three long weeks working at SBB Engineering and I was slowly losing the will to live. Three weeks of my life that I'd never be able to get back. When Polly had offered me the new assignment I'd made sure to quiz her on whether the role would require any dressing up in ridiculous costumes. When she'd assured me it didn't, I'd jumped at the opportunity. My priority, I realised, had to be to earn as much money as I possibly could, especially as the Christmas season was approaching, to supplement my freelance income and enable me to do all the exciting things I wanted to do.

Instead of being thrown into a stimulating and challenging new environment with dynamic new people, as I'd hoped and expected, I was stuck alone, in a top floor office of a company that sourced and supplied ball bearings.

The tiny office had only a small window which, slightly worryingly, had bars against it, a single desk and chair and hundreds of box files that seemed to date back to pre-millennium times – stacked in dangerous Jenga-style piles around the room, just waiting to topple over and pin me to the floor. On the windowsill was a forlorn pot plant that I took it upon myself to nurture back to health. In the absence of anyone else to talk to, I gave it a few encouraging words each day and some much overdue water.

'Hello, how's it going?' Kelly, the office manager, the only other person I'd met since I'd started at SBB, poked her head round the door. She was friendly in a forced, unnatural way, which made me suspect she actually hated me beneath the cheery persona. She'd spoken of Bob and Michael and sales directors and 'the team', but I hadn't actually seen another soul and I was beginning to wonder if they weren't all a figment of her imagination and this wasn't just a one-woman operation.

'Great' I said, opting not to tell her that I was close to slitting my wrists at the sheer mind-numbing drudgery of the task in front of me. 'Slowly, but I'm getting there.'

'Yes.' She peered over my shoulder at the computer print-outs on my desk, I could feel her disappointment wafting over me in a low cloud of gloom. 'We were hoping you might be a bit further along than you are, but hopefully you'll speed up as you get more used to the product details.'

I sighed inwardly, feeling I already knew far more about ball bearings than I really needed to know: stainless steel, chrome, quarter inch, half inch, miniature, deep groove, self-aligning, super precision, packs of fifty, packs of a thousand and everything in between. I typed in that many entries into the new order processing system I felt sure I could have chosen ball bearings as my specialist subject on Mastermind and come out with the winning score.

'When you're done with those ones I've got some additional product details that need to be added here.' She handed me a great fat wedge of print-outs, twice the size of the ones I'd entered already. The sight of them sent me lightheaded. At this rate I'd be here until my dying day, possibly crushed to death under the weight of all those files.

'Fine,' I said, smiling sweetly. 'I'll get on to them as soon as I can.' My mobile phone buzzed on the desk and I reached across to see who it was.

'Oh,' she said haughtily, 'perhaps I should have mentioned it, Jen, but I'm afraid you're not allowed to take personal calls here.'

'Excuse me?'

'Nothing personal, you understand, but it's company policy. I'd be grateful if you could put your phone away until your allocated break time.'

Ten minutes at 10.50, half an hour at lunch to be taken between 12.30 and 13.00, and ten minutes at 15.20. My life had become regulated by breaks and ball bearings in such a short space of time.

On my phone I could see a text message from Angie mocking me. Flashing at me insistently, urging me to tell Kelly to jog on and hurry up and pick up the message. I could almost hear Angie's laughter permeating the room. I turned round and faced Kelly.

'I haven't actually used my phone since I've been here, but I do like to have it at hand just in case there is an emergency at home. My granddad has been very ill and my best friend is about to give birth so I think you'll understand why I feel the need to keep my phone close by.'

Kelly took a deep breath and clasped her hands in front of her as though she was about to deliver a sermon.

'In those circumstances what we suggest you do is give the main switchboard number to your friends and family and then if there is such an emergency they can contact you that way. Otherwise, what we've found is that people, especially those working unsupervised, can abuse the time they're supposed to be working here by texting their friends, going onto Facebook and scouring the internet. You'd be surprised at how much company time is lost through such things. Obviously, I'm not suggesting you would do that, but you know, just to be on the safe side, I would be grateful if you could respect our company policy and put the phone away.'

Her mouth smiled sweetly but everything else remained coolly disdainful.

My phone, as though it had been listening to this whole conversation, leapt into action again, this time its insistent ringing made Kelly's over-manicured eyebrows arch skywards. Angie was impatient at the best of times, but today especially so. I grabbed the phone and stabbed at the green button, much to Kelly's dismay.

'Angie?'

'Jen! There you are! I've been trying to get hold of you. I think it's started. I think I'm going into labour.'

'What? Nooo! You can't, can you? Not today. Isn't it too early?'

'I know that, but try telling that to the sprog. I've got pains, Jen. Really bad ones. Can you come over?'

'I'll be straight there. Hang on! Do some puffing and blowing or whatever it is you're supposed to do.'

I hung up and grabbed my handbag from the floor, before turning to Kelly, who was hovering beside me like an impatient bumblebee.

'Sorry, I'm going to have to go.'

'But it's only three o'clock. You're never going to finish those entries if you pop out now.'

'No, you're absolutely right,' I said, with a couldn't-care-less shrug of my shoulders.

'Well, when will you be back exactly?' The hackles were clearly visible on the back of her neck.

I glanced at my watch, my gaze travelling round the little room and landing on the poor little pot plant that was looking as worn down and defeated as I was feeling.

'I won't, I'm afraid.' There had to be some perks to temping and I'd just discovered the biggest one of them all. I didn't care what Kelly thought and I didn't care what Polly thought. Life was far too short to be worrying about ball bearings. 'I won't be coming back.'

'What, today?'

'Nope. Nor tomorrow. Or any other day come to that. Sorry. I've had enough of this job. Ball bearings aren't really my thing, I'm afraid.'

I waltzed out of the door and was three steps down the stairs when I remembered something I'd forgotten. I ran back upstairs, past Kelly who was standing there looking as though she was still trying to figure out what had just happened, and into the office – snatching the little pot plant from the windowsill. I couldn't bear the thought of leaving it behind, alone and forlorn, in that miserable office. Like me, all it needed was the opportunity to flourish and grow.

'I'll take this with me, if you don't mind,' I said breezily, not hanging around long enough to hear whether she did or not.

* * *

I sprinted to the car park, jumped in my car and zoomed through the streets of Casterton, cursing at anyone who had the audacity to get in my way. I just hoped to goodness I wouldn't be too late. What if she'd already given birth at home on the kitchen floor? My stomach churned. I really hoped not – I wasn't great with blood and the thought of all that mess made me regret the oozing pulled pork roll I'd had for my lunch. I took a shortcut through

Manor Road, avoiding the high street, but quickly came to a grinding halt behind a white transit van that had decided to stop in the middle of the road, its back doors flung open.

The driver had climbed into the back of the van and was rummaging through his parcels as though he had all the time in the world. I tapped on the steering wheel, trying to remain calm, but the longer he faffed about the more I could feel my blood pressure rising. I wound down the window and poked my head out.

'Are you going to be long? It's just that I'm in a bit of a hurry.'

'Only doing my job, love. A couple of minutes at the most.'

I wound the window up seething, absolutely furious that he could think his time was so much more important than mine. What was it with men and their overriding sense of entitlement? I could just imagine Mr White Van Man's reaction if I'd done the same to him. He'd have been tooting on his horn and calling me every name under the sun. I sighed and looked into my rear view mirror. This was ridiculous. Now there was a queue of traffic lining up behind me so there was absolutely no means of escape. I beeped my horn three times in quick succession, a car behind me joining in with the melody.

When White Van Man simply laughed and waved, clearly taking great pleasure in my growing annoyance I leapt out of my car and confronted him.

'Look, move your bloody van now,' I said, channelling my inner bear. 'I've been called out on a medical emergency. I should be assisting at the birth of a child right now, not waiting on you to get your arse into gear. Show a bit of consideration by parking in a place that's not going to hold up all the traffic.' I gestured towards all the cars behind me just in case he was missing my point. 'There is a frightened and vulnerable pregnant woman waiting on me and if anything should happen to her whilst I'm stuck here then I'm going to hold you personally responsible. I've taken a note of your registration number. Do you understand?'

'I'm really sorry, love,' he said, having the good grace to look sheepish as he slammed the doors of the van shut. 'You should have said. I'm on my way now. You ought to have a flashing light on your car, you know that. Then you wouldn't have these problems.'

'Yes, well, thank you.' I wasn't sure about a flashing light but I felt certain my face was shining a lovely shade of shameful scarlet. 'I'll remember that for next time.'

Five minutes later I pulled up outside Angie and Tom's little cottage and rushed up to the front door, banging urgently on the knocker.

'Jen! Ooh, how lovely to see you,' said Angie, as if me turning up was a total surprise. She wafted to the threshold in a cream floaty dress, her skin and hair glowing with vitality and health, her whole being exuding serenity and calm, whilst I grabbed onto the door handle gasping for breath, convinced I might pass out at any moment.

'What's happening? Have you called the doctor? How close are the contractions?'

'Oh that,' she giggled, waving her arm in the air nonchalantly, 'that was a false alarm. Apparently it's quite common in the last few weeks. Still, it's so lovely you're here. Come inside and we can have a good old catch-up.'

20

I was slumped in Angie's armchair, my nerves completely frazzled.

'You do realise I walked out on my job to come dashing to your side, Angie. I was panicking. From what you said, I thought the baby might have arrived by the time I got here.'

Angie handed me a big mug of tea and a plate of biscuits which went a small way to making me feel marginally better after my mad dash across town and my run-in with Kelly and White Van Man.

'Sorry, Jen. I kind of forget that there's still a whole other world going on out there. I've been lost in my own little pregnancy bubble. Do you think you ought to get back to work then?'

'No, don't worry. I walked out for good.' Angie's face fell, but I was quick to reassure her. 'Really, you did me a favour. It was officially the worst job in the world and I was looking for an excuse to leave. Your false alarm gave me that. I'll give the agency a call later and explain.'

'Are you missing working at Browns?'

'In some ways. I miss the people, Matt, our lovely customers, but I was well overdue a change. Besides, I'm committed now to getting my own business off the ground, it's given me something else to focus on and I'm really enjoying having different projects on the go. My social media presence is growing all the time, I've been asked to write some gardening features for an in-house magazine and there's a possibility of me running a few work-shops down at the local arts centre too.'

'Blimey, Jen, you sound busier than ever. I'm really proud of you.' She grimaced, as she fought with the cushion on her chair, attempting to make herself more comfortable. She took a sip of her chamomile tea and looked across at me. 'Tom mentioned he ran into you and Alex the other night. What's going on between you two?'

'Me and Tom? Nothing.' I cringed inwardly, wondering what exactly he'd told her. 'We didn't really chat for long, just said hello and then we were on our way.'

'Honestly, Jen, anyone would think it was you who was pregnant. Your head is all over the place. No, not Tom. I meant you and Alex. What's happening with you two?'

'Oh,' I smiled with relief. From her reaction I was guessing Tom hadn't mentioned our little disagreement which was prob-ably a good thing. I didn't want there to be any awkwardness between us the next time we all got together.

'We've been out a few times that's all.' I realised a big smile had spread involuntarily across my face and, I suspected, a dreamy expression too, so I quickly rearranged my features into something more perfunctory, but Angie wasn't being fooled.

'Oh God, you like him, don't you? You really like him. I can tell.'

'Yes, he seems like a decent guy actually.' I wasn't going to make any apologies to Angie. Not now I knew her little secret. The one she hadn't chosen to share with me. The one about her having her own particular soft spot for Alex. 'He's lovely. Perfect date material, and he certainly knows how to treat a woman. We're enjoying each other's company and having a good time. That's all. He's got me back into that whole dating scene. I was so out of practice before.'

Despite sounding in control, I knew I was in much deeper than I'd ever intended to be. Alex occupied my every waking thought. Seeing his name on my phone, hearing his voice, spending time with him over a drink sent butterflies flittering the length of my body, stirring a craving within me for more, much more of Alex. I loved his worldliness, the fact that he seemed to know something about everything and I loved the way he didn't take himself or life too seriously either. The fact that he was probably the most gorgeous man I'd ever set eyes on was just an added bonus.

I gulped, realising I loved pretty much everything about him, but most of all I loved the way he seemed infinitely charmed and amused by me; those deep intense eyes, full of warmth and kindness, were forever appraising me, and the acceptance I recognised in those eyes melted my heart.

I shook my head to rid myself of the soppy thoughts. It was as if I'd been struck by some virulent disease and my immunity was at an all-time low. Was it time to extract myself from this fledgling relationship? I suspected I would probably be going the same way as a dozen other girls before me. I needed to leave with some dignity intact before Alex crushed my heart into a tiny dozen pieces.

'Yes, I admit he's perfect date material, but I'm not so sure he's perfect boyfriend material,' said Angie. 'But don't say I didn't warn you.'

'You did warn me, Angie, but do you know something, apart from you saying he's a bit of a ladies' man, I can't really see why you were quite so anti us getting together. I know I'm out of practice when it comes to men, but I'm a grown woman. I'm quite capable of looking after myself, you know.'

She glanced across at me and I could see she was taken aback by the sharpness of my unexpected reply.

'It wasn't that I was anti you two getting together, I just didn't want you to get hurt, that's all,' she said, dropping her gaze to twiddle her thumbs in her lap. 'You have to remember I know what he's like, I've seen the way he treats women.'

I raised my eyebrows at her, chewing on the inside of my cheek, wondering whether I shouldn't just let it go. But I'd heard Alex's side of the story. I needed to hear Angie's now. 'Not so badly that you weren't interested in him yourself at one time?'

She snapped her attention onto my face. 'What do you mean?'

'Alex said you two had a bit of a flirtation at one time. Is that right?'

'Oh, the bastard! So much for him being a gentleman. He promised me he wouldn't say anything. It was embarrassing, a one-off. If Tom ever finds out, he'll go absolutely mad.'

'Don't be silly! Alex would never say anything and neither would I. It was just that he was pressing me on why I had such strong views about the sort of person he was and I had to admit they kind of came from you.'

Our eyes locked together and we giggled and I knew immediately she was forgiven, if I'd ever had anything to be cross with her about in the first place.

'Oh God,' she said, dropping her head in her hands. 'I feel awful now. I was never seriously interested in Alex in that way. I promise you! It was when Tom and I were on one of our breaks, before you'd even met Alex, and I was at a low ebb. I might even have been a little drunk too. I thought a flirtation with Alex might give me a lift, but he wasn't having any of it. Honestly, can you imagine what that did to my ego? Alex has had a whole string of girlfriends, I thought he'd jump at the chance of a fling, but he didn't want anything to do with it. Mind you, I realise now it was a good job one of us had some sense. If anything had happened it would have made things very awkward between Tom and me.'

'Angie, I just wish you'd said something to me.'

'Sorry,' she said, with a sheepish grin. 'I just felt embarrassed by that whole episode. It wasn't that I didn't want you to have him because I couldn't have him for myself or anything like that. You have to believe that. No really!' she protested, seeing my wide-eyed reaction. 'I suppose I was just worried that you would fall madly in love with him and end up hurt.'

I nodded. That had been exactly my worry too.

'So come on, tell me then, what's going on between the pair of you? Are you officially a couple now?'

'No, nothing like that. It's funny though, I keep running into him.' Was that simply coincidence or fate lending a hand? 'We've been out on a few dates and always have a great time, but I suppose there's a part of me that's been holding back, waiting for the inevitable to happen.' I grimaced, making a slashing motion against my neck, making Angie laugh.

'Look, maybe I haven't been very fair towards Alex,' said Angie, examining her fingernails. 'I'm sure with the right woman he'd make the perfect partner. I just don't know if the perfect woman for him exists out there. Mind you, I think I probably have a lot to be thankful to Alex for at the moment. He took Tom out to dinner the other night and I'm not sure what it was he said to him but Tom's been much more attentive ever since.'

'Really?' I said, feigning nonchalance. 'How come?'

'Well, he came home from seeing Alex and we had a bit of a heart-to-heart. He admitted that he'd found it a shock when he first realised I was pregnant and that he'd struggled to come to terms with the idea, but he told me how much he loved me and he apologised for acting like a complete idiot at times.'

'Wow! Well, that's good. Perhaps he's beginning to realise what marriage is all about and how lucky he is to have you and your unborn baby.'

'Yes, I think it was quite brave of him actually. To admit to those feelings. I think he was frightened that everything was going to change and he didn't seem to have any control over that, but we've talked it through and I think we're in a much better place now. He's agreed to make sure he leaves work on time at least a couple of nights a week. And we're going to make Sunday a family day when we get to do something together. Tom's really looking forward to the baby arriving now and I'm feeling much happier and more confident about the future.'

'I'm really pleased about that, Angie.' Could Alex really have said something that had made Tom stop and think about the way he was behaving? Or perhaps my little rant had hit a nerve with him after all. Either way, it didn't really matter. As long as Tom and Angie were getting on better then that was everything.

'Fancy another cuppa?' said Angie, as she eased herself out of the chair. 'I just need to pop to the loo and then I'll put the kettle on, I seem to spend my whole life in there these days. Ooh, could you get that for me?' she asked, hearing the doorbell ring.

I walked down the hallway, feeling relieved that everything was out in the open now. I opened the door and smiled, taking the package from the delivery man.

'Oh, hello love, how's it going?' It was Mr White Van Man, looking much bigger, much broader and altogether more scary up close. He craned his neck to look behind me. 'Has that baby arrived yet?'

'Ah yes, sorry about that, it was something of a false alarm, I'm afraid.' I almost felt guilty that I didn't have a baby in my arms to show him, but thankfully Angie took that moment to waddle out, giving some credence to my story.

'Actually, Jen, I'm not sure it was a false alarm.' She was standing, legs apart, looking unbelievingly at the small pool of water forming a puddle at her feet. 'Either I've wet myself or my waters have just broken.'

'Oh my god, what does that mean?' My voice came out in a strangulated cry.

'Blimey! Is this your first time or something, love?' said White Van Man to me. 'I'm not a health professional but even I know what that means. You need to get your rubber gloves on and the towels out, and look a bit lively. Do you want me to stay and help?'

'No!' Angie and I said together firmly, as he was already rolling his sleeves up, a gleeful look on his face. 'We'll be absolutely fine.'

We scooped up Angie's belongings that were all packed up and ready to go by the front door, and rushed, as much as a heavily pregnant woman can rush, to the car. The journey to the hospital went at a much more sedate pace than the mad dash I'd made from work as I was conscious of Angie sitting beside me wincing every time we went over a bump.

'You are all right, aren't you?' I said, peering at her in the passenger seat as she pulled all sorts of faces. 'Please darling, I love you dearly, but don't have this baby in my car.'

Angie managed to giggle through the heavy breathing. 'Stop panicking. I'm fine. For a woman in labour. Just get me to the hospital. Did you put my bags in the back of the car?'

'Yes. And I spoke to Tom too. He was already on his way home so he said he'd go straight to the hospital and meet us there.'

'I still can't believe this is actually happening,' sighed Angie. She cradled her bump in her arms. 'To think that when I go back to the house again I'll be taking a baby with me. It's surreal. I'm so glad you're here with me though.' She reached out a hand to me. 'I wouldn't have wanted to take this trip on my own. Actually there's something I want to ask you, Jen, and I don't know why I haven't asked you before. Would you stay with me for the birth? Be my birth partner? It would mean the world to me.'

I felt the blood drain from my face and a peculiar feeling of lightheadedness come over me. 'Really? Well, of course... If you'd like me to. I just thought, with it being your first child, you'd want it to be just you and Tom.'

Angie had her lips pursed together before bursting out with laughter.

'Ha ha, your face! I really had you going there, didn't I? No, darling, you're off the hook. I love you dearly but I wouldn't want you there at the birth of my child because I wouldn't want to see your worried face looking at me the whole time. You'd be panicking and that would only make me worry more. No, at least I can rely on Tom to be totally unfazed and laid back about the whole thing. That's if he turns up!'

Relief slumped through my shoulders. I didn't want to be Angie's birth partner, or anyone else's come to that. In fact, if I could arrange it so that I wouldn't need to be present at the births of my own babies, I would. Of course I would have agreed to stay with Angie if she'd wanted me to, but I really didn't relish the thought of seeing my friend suffer so much pain and discomfort. I'd much rather cheer from the sidelines, or more pertinently, the pub.

'Of course he'll be there!' And if he wasn't, I'd physically go and find him, and drag him there screaming and kicking, if necessary. Anything to ensure I wouldn't have to be his stand-in.

21

Thankfully that wasn't necessary as when we arrived at the hospital Tom was waiting outside, looking incredibly nervous while practising his pacing up and down routine. My heart lifted to see Alex with him, a strange mix of affection and desire filling every fibre of my body.

'Do you think we should go and wet the baby's head?' asked Alex, after we'd seen Angie and Tom off into the maternity suite, wishing them the best of luck.

'Aren't you supposed to do that after the baby's born?'

'Yeah, but there's no harm in starting early. Besides, from what I've heard this labour lark can be a long and drawn out process. We're going to need some sustenance to see us through.'

We found it in the form of a very nice bottle of Chablis and a steak burger, oozing cheese and mushrooms and thousands of calories I didn't doubt, along with a portion of chunky chips in a lovely little gastro pub in town. We sat in cosy armchairs next to a wood-burning stove and a sense of euphoria engulfed me. My stomach was full, my head was light, I no longer had to go and sit in that grotty little office, my best friend was about to give birth and a gorgeous man was sitting opposite me, smiling fondly. Could it get any better than this?

'Angie was saying that Tom is a changed man these days, and apparently it all came about after meeting up with you the other night. What on earth did you say to him?'

Alex smiled in that way of his that suggested he knew something I didn't, which always spoke directly to the depths of my stomach. 'Oh, you know, it was just one of those man-to-man things. To be honest, I think you had him worried after your run-in with him. We did have a bit of a heart-to-heart. He asked me what I thought and if you might have a point or not.'

'And what did you say?'

'I said it didn't really matter what you or I thought, it was how he and Angie felt about things that mattered. I think it was the first time he'd stopped to think about the enormity of what they'd done. Getting married, moving in together and having a baby, it all happened in such a short space of time and to be honest, I think he found it a little overwhelming. He adores Angie though, that much I do know and he's desperate not to mess things up this time. I think those conversations we had with him made him stop and think. He wants to be a good dad to their new baby and, do you know, I think he will be. I think he's done a lot of growing up in these last few months.'

'Yes, maybe it's just taken him a little time to get used to the idea.'

'He's a lucky guy. And I told him that, but I also told him he couldn't afford to take things for granted. You can't go into a marriage with everything that entails and not give it a hundred per cent. Otherwise, what's the point?'

'Exactly.' I smiled, pleased that Alex and I were on the same page. I picked up my cappuccino, taking a sip from the frothy topping. 'Listen to us. Sitting here as though we're experts on love and marriage.'

'Well, it doesn't seem that difficult to me.'

'Doesn't it? You've admitted most of your relationships have been short-term affairs. How can you possibly know the first thing about love and marriage? To me it seems like one of the most difficult things you can do in life. How do you know if the other person is the right one for you? When do you know if you're ready to make that next step to something more permanent, more lasting? How do you know if you can make it work together? There are so many questions and yet there can be no definitive answers.'

I thought I'd had all the answers with Paul, but sadly it hadn't turned out the way I'd expected it to. I'd been left with a bruised heart and so many unanswered questions, wondering how I could have got everything quite so wrong.

Now Alex narrowed his eyes at me, his mouth chewing thoughtfully on my words. 'I think when you meet that special one then you just know. Deep down in here.' He banged his fist on his chest. 'And then it isn't a difficult decision at all. You just have to take a chance.'

'Is that what you're holding out for then?'

'Yep, it is actually,' he said, fixing me with a determined gaze. And just biding his time with me and a whole load of other girls, I didn't doubt, in the meantime. Is that all I was to him? A diversion, someone to spend a few enjoyable nights with until he met that special girl? I looked away. I couldn't bring myself to hold the intensity of his gaze, it was far too intimate and intrusive, and hugely disconcerting as well. 'What's so wrong with that?'

'Nothing.' Of course there wasn't anything wrong with that. And why I should feel unsettled by his honesty I didn't know. I'd known exactly what I was getting into when I first hooked up with Alex. Angie had warned me and Alex had admitted himself he didn't do long-term relationships. Friends with benefits, isn't that what they called it. Only how could I have known the benefits were much more addictive and compelling than I could ever have imagined.

'I was in a long-term relationship once. I do know what that's all about.'

'Really?' I looked at him closely across the table, my curiosity piqued.

'Yes, don't sound so surprised. Admittedly it was a long time ago now, but I have been there.'

'What happened?' I asked, intrigued.

His brow furrowed, a deep groove settling in the spot between his eyes, which was a much safer place to focus on, I decided.

'It ended badly. We were childhood sweethearts. Her parents were great friends of my parents so we kind of grew up together. Went to the same school together, had the same friends, shared birthdays and Christmases. It was kind of inevitable that we would become an item.'

'Wow! That sounds pretty intense. How long were you together for?'

'About five years. We got together when we were fourteen and split when we were nineteen.'

'Why did you break up then? Did you just outgrow each other?'

'Kind of. We got engaged. Had the big party and then... well basically I realised I didn't want to be engaged. I was far too young. I certainly didn't want to be thinking about marriage. I was nineteen and I suddenly woke up to a whole other world out there. I wanted to go travelling, date other girls, basically catch up on all those things I'd been missing out on in my teenage years. You can imagine, it didn't go down too well with my folks or with Clare's family. And, to my great regret, I broke Clare's heart.'

'Oh no, that's hard.' I could imagine exactly how poor Clare might have felt.

'It was and of course I became public enemy number one.'

'But it was hardly your fault.' I shrugged my shoulders. Nineteen was far too young to know what it was you wanted from life. I was only coming to grips with that now. 'No one could blame you for breaking up with your childhood sweetheart, not in those circumstances. I can understand you wanting to break free and getting some life experience.'

'People did blame me though and sadly Clare took it hard. She was very hurt and it affected her badly. She became depressed and had a breakdown. She was even hospitalised for a short while and I know it took her a couple of years to get her life back on track. It damaged the relationship between our two families which had always been very close before. They don't speak at all now.'

'Oh no. That's awful.' I was seeing a different side to Alex, an altogether softer, more vulnerable side. He was opening up to me in a way that I could never have expected.

'Yeah, when I look back at that time I wonder if I could have done things differently. For a long time I beat myself up about it for putting everyone, Clare especially, through so much heartbreak. I don't know if there was some other way I could have done it, a way where I could have avoided hurting Clare but I don't think so. That's why I've never wanted to make the same mistake again, Jen.' He picked up my hand from across the table and gave a small smile. 'After what happened with Clare, I told myself I wouldn't make any promises or get too involved with anyone, not unless I knew it was going to be something significant, something meaningful. Do you understand what I'm saying, Jen?'

'Oh yes. Of course I understand,' I said airily, as though we shared exactly the same intention. I paused and took a deep breath, I was picking up on Alex's message loud and clear.

'This is your five-minute warning. If you want to get out of here with your heart intact, please leave the vicinity immediately.'

It wasn't difficult to understand what he was trying to tell me. It was what I'd already known. That he wasn't interested in a serious relationship, he was just out for a good time and I could have no cause to take exception to that fact because he'd been nothing but honest with me from the start. Clare had been the unlucky one. She'd had her heart well and truly broken, and Alex was warning me that I shouldn't allow it to happen to me.

I took my hand away and glanced at my watch, wondering how Angie was doing. She was on the brink of a brand new stage in her life and I was overjoyed for her, but my mood felt dampened now by Alex's words. What had I been expecting? I'd been telling myself since that very first day I met him not to have any expectations, but all the time the words had been left unsaid there was a sense of anticipation and excitement bubbling inside me. A hope, I realised now, of something more. Alex would be so easy to fall in love with and I'd had a very close call there.

'Sorry,' said Alex, 'I don't know where that came from. I rarely talk to anyone about those times, I hope you don't mind me offloading all of that on you.'

'No, not at all. I'm glad you told me.'

Actually it made a lot of sense. Laying out the rules before you got too involved with someone. Letting people know where you stood. In theory, it made absolute sense but in practice I wasn't certain it worked at all.

'Crikey, is that the time? I really ought to get home. It's been a long day and I know I won't get much sleep tonight waiting on a text from Tom or Angie to come through.' I pulled out my credit card and placed it on the bill.

'No, absolutely not. This is my treat. You can take me out some other time. How about that?'

I raised my eyebrows and shrugged. Would there be another time? What was it Alex had told me the other night? Something about there being no point in hanging around if you knew a relationship wasn't going anywhere.

'Thanks, Alex,' I said with a cool smile. I had to give it to him, he was an expert at dating, but then I supposed he'd had plenty of practice. He was kind and courteous and generous, all of those things and many more. Everything a girl would want in a date and a boyfriend, come to that.

Outside, he put an arm around my waist, pulling me into his side. I was beginning to wonder if he selected his aftershave purely for its seductive properties. His scent was intoxicating and his touch sent a delicious nugget of anticipation swirling around my stomach. His lips hovered teasingly close to my mouth and despite everything I knew about this man I couldn't help myself from standing on tiptoes to kiss him, his mouth responding instinctively to mine. I kissed him, as if we were discovering each other for the first time, biting, nibbling, exploring, not caring for a moment that we were standing in the middle of the high street, nor worrying who might see us like that, like two lovestruck teenagers. I wanted to consign his delectable taste to my memory so that I would never forget the exquisiteness of his kisses. He pulled away, running a hand along the side of my face, his eyes devouring me in their usual hungry manner.

'Look, let's get a taxi back to mine, you can't drive, not after what we've had to drink tonight. I can bring you down in the morning to collect your car.'

Thoughtful, so very thoughtful, but with an eye for the main chance, obviously. I didn't need anyone else to tell me that, I was quite capable of working out just what Alex was like for myself.

'Actually, I'm going straight home. I've got a few jobs I need to do. It's been a lovely evening, Alex, but I really have to go.' I just needed to hang onto the tiny bit of resolve I had left.

'Don't go, Jen. I really want to be with you tonight. More than anything. Come back with me. Please.' His thumb stroked my cheek, his breath warm against my ear, his other hand finding my waist and a shiver of desire ran down the length of my body.

Was this how all those other girls had felt? Swept off their feet, full of hope and desire not just for the night ahead, but for some kind of future with this undoubtedly gorgeous man. I didn't want to go the way of teardrop earring girl, here one day and then her memory consigned to some forgotten jewellery on a bedside cabinet.

I kissed him again, just as fervently, just as urgently. I kissed him as though it were for the last time. 'Sorry Alex, I really have to go.'

This dating lark was easy as long as you just remembered a few ground rules.

22

Tom and Angie would be delighted if you could join us to celebrate
the Christening Day
of our daughter
Liberty Rose
on Sunday 21st February at 11.30 a.m.
at St Barnabas Chapel, Casterton

'Hi Jen, fancy seeing you here!' Alex Fellows winked at me and
my heart, despite me giving it a stern talking to beforehand,
treacherously went pitter patter, pitter patter. 'You are looking
absolutely gorgeous as always.'

'Why thank you!' I said, accepting his kiss on my cheek with
feigned coolness, catching a whiff of his familiar aftershave in the
process. I'd seen him a couple of times briefly since the night of
Liberty's birth, mainly around at Angie and Tom's.

Now, we were standing in the grounds of St Barnabas Chapel,
following a beautiful service celebrating the christening of our
dear little goddaughter, Liberty. The morning sunshine was

making a valiant attempt at breaking through the trees and cast a warmly benevolent glow over the proceedings.

Inside the church, I'd made a concerted effort not to catch Alex's eye. I was fully aware of his surreptitious gaze upon me, but I'd been determined to fix all my attention on Angie and Tom, and their beautiful baby.

'How lovely to see you.' I plastered on my best smile. Even if I'd wanted to avoid Alex for the rest of my life I was beginning to realise that might not be realistic. Thanks to Angie and Tom, our lives would always be inextricably linked – birthdays, Christmases, barbecues, all those Cooper family celebrations to come, and I felt sure there would be a lot of them, occasions where our paths were bound to cross.

If I'd hoped that putting some distance between us might lessen the strength of my feelings towards him then I'd been very much mistaken. His proximity could still turn my legs to jelly even after all these weeks.

'We're getting very good at this, aren't we? Weddings, births, funerals. You know we could consider renting ourselves out as professional guests.'

I laughed. 'That's not a bad idea.'

Angie and Tom spotted us and came over to join us, their faces alight with happiness and pride.

'Jen and Alex, I just wanted to say a huge thank you for being here today.' Angie slipped her arms around our waists while Tom stood to one side cradling Liberty. 'I can't tell you how much it means to us to have you two, our very best friends, as godparents to our precious little girl.'

'I see it as a great honour,' said Alex. 'I will take it upon myself to teach this young lady everything she needs to know about rugby, real ales, fine wines and fine art. As you know, I'm an expert in these things.'

'Poor child,' I said, with a rueful grin. 'And it'll be my duty to ensure that she isn't bored senseless by her godfather's outlandish tales.'

'I know you're not impressed by me and my worldly ways, Jen, but I think this little lady will have much better taste than you and will come to adore her Uncle Alex.' He chastised me with a look and I didn't doubt for a moment that it would be a mutual admiration society as far as these two were concerned. 'Come on,' he said to Tom, growing impatient now, 'I think it must be my turn for a cuddle.'

Talk about smitten. Tom handed over Liberty Rose wrapped in an intricate white lace shawl, placing her carefully into Alex's arms, and Alex's face lit up, a picture of wonder. There was no hesitancy in his movement, only a natural affinity with the tiny bundle in his arms as he gently ran a finger over her cheek, undeniable adoration in his eyes. I'd been on the receiving end of one of those looks before, the reminder making my stomach swirl deliciously and viewing it from any angle made me realise just how hard it was to stay immune to Alex's charms for any length of time.

Tom dragged Angie away to speak to some guests and Alex and I were left literally holding the baby.

'Wouldn't you love one of these?' Alex said, rocking Liberty in his arms.

'Not right at the moment, thank you,' I said with a smile and his eyes hooked onto mine, that undeniable fizzing chemistry rearing its head again. It was weird, but even when I hadn't seen Alex in a while, we always quickly picked up where we left off. It made me realise just how much I'd missed him, how much I enjoyed his company. I peered over to examine Liberty, marvelling at her utter perfection. 'To be honest, I've not had a lot of experience of small children. They scare me a bit. I worry that I'm going to drop them or hurt them in some way.'

'Really? That surprises me. They're very resilient you know. I can't wait to have kids of my own. It's what life is all about, don't you think? Family, friends?'

I nodded my agreement, but for some reason felt unsettled by the intimacy of the conversation. 'I guess so.'

Alex passed the baby into my arms and, much more awkwardly, I jiggled her up and down hoping to goodness she wouldn't do anything that might require me to look as though I knew what I was doing. 'I'm hoping Tom and Angie are going to give me a crash course in baby care before they ask me to do any babysitting duties. Or else I won't have a clue as to what I'm supposed to do with this little one.'

'Oh, there's nothing to it, Jen. Kids don't come with an instruction manual. You just make it up as you go along. And go with the flow.'

He made it sound so easy and I suspected, with Alex, it would be. I could imagine him as a father; very hands-on, capable and confident, always knowing exactly the right thing to do.

'You know what your trouble is, don't you, Jen?'

'No, but I think you're about to tell me.'

'Well, just an observation from one friend to another.'

I raised my eyebrows at him and grimaced, bracing myself for what he might have to say.

'You think too much about things.'

I gave a wry smile, wondering if he'd be on the hotline up to my mum.

'I can see your mind working overtime. Weighing up whether something is a good idea or not. Sometimes you just have to take a chance on new ideas, new adventures, new situations and give them a try, see where they take you.'

Yep, he'd definitely been in cahoots with my mum.

'So basically,' I said, 'you're saying I'm an uptight repressed woman who needs to learn how to enjoy herself. Is that it?'

'No, not at all.' Alex laughed, taking the baby from me again. He positioned her on his shoulder, tapping her back lightly as he swayed on the spot. 'But just think if I'd given you a choice about going zip-lining, you would never have agreed to go in the first place. But you did it and had a great time.'

'It wasn't that great a time,' I said, churlishly. 'The best thing about it was getting to the other side and realising I was still alive. That was a good feeling. A great feeling even, but I mean, I would never want to do that again.'

'Oh Jen! You said you wanted to find some adventure in your life and that's what that day was all about. It should have shown you just what you're capable of. I think deep down in your heart you're far more adventurous than you give yourself credit for. Giving up your job, going it alone, that's pretty adventurous.'

'I suppose.'

We were interrupted by another christening guest who was all too eager to have a cuddle with the baby and Alex duly passed her on, albeit reluctantly. He slipped his arm through mine and we wandered off, coming to a halt at a secluded spot out of the way under a yew tree.

'I quite like your uptightness though, even if I do find it incredibly frustrating.'

'Alex,' I said, elbowing him surreptitiously in the ribs. 'What do you mean?'

'You know what I mean. Why have you been avoiding me again, Jen?' He turned to face me. We were standing so close I could feel his breath on my face. 'I thought we were getting on really well, I imagined that you liked me, Jen. Christ, I really like you. Don't you realise that? I haven't stopped thinking about you from the first day we met and I thought, well I'd hoped that we would carry on seeing each other, getting to know each other better. But just as I think we're moving forward, you blow me out again. What's that all about? Did I just misread the signs, Jen? Is that it?'

I looked down at our hands entwined, our bodies as close together as they could possibly be without actually touching, and I wondered how that had actually happened. I couldn't remember our hands finding each other. The underlying tension between us was palpable. There could be no mistaking the signs.

'Alex, we shouldn't be talking about this now. This is our godchild's christening. Look, people are making a move to go back to the house. We should go.'

He put a hand onto the small of my back and guided me through the grounds of the chapel before we joined the alleyway that ran the short distance to Tom and Angie's house, walking together in silence.

When we reached the cottage we found the house festooned with balloons and ribbons, and inside in the open plan living area Angie's imposing pine dresser was overflowing with pink wrapped presents and gift bags, the happy sounds of laughter ringing out from all around. On the dining room table the most wonderful buffet had been laid out and bottles of pink champagne stood ready to be cracked open.

With glass in hand and suitably filled, I mooched around the room catching up with people, some I hadn't seen since the wedding. I had a chat and a giggle with Gladys and Betty, had another cuddle with Liberty, which felt slightly more comfortable this time, and had an extended hug too with Angie, who seemed to have taken to motherhood with inherent ease. Yet I supposed I should have realised it was an inevitability that Alex and I would find ourselves together again, irresistibly drawn to one another like magnets, huddled beside each other on the small sofa at the front of the house, nestled into the bay window, the warm sun caressing our backs.

'Can I ask you a personal question?' Alex said, turning to me with serious intent in his eyes.

I gulped. 'Yes, of course, what is it?'

'Are you seeing someone else?'

The directness of his question took me by surprise and I took another sip of pink champagne to fortify me.

'No,' I said, equally directly.

'Okay, good. It was just I wondered about you and that guy from work, is it Matt? I thought I'd check. Didn't want to be stepping on anyone's toes.'

'No, nothing like that. Matt's just a friend.'

'Okay, good,' he said again, and I couldn't help noticing that he actually looked relieved, very relieved. 'So give it to me straight, Jen? What is it that you don't like about me or us? I know there's something stopping you, holding you back from getting involved with me. I've sensed that from the beginning and I just wish I knew what it was because then I might be able to do something to fix it. Do you see me just as a friend and nothing more, is that it? For me, every time we're together it's incredible. I thought that first night after the wedding was amazing, but then last time when you stayed over, it was even better. When we're together, it's great and I'm certain you feel that way too, but then just when I feel we're growing closer you blow me out again. I don't get it. Do you really not feel the same way too?'

'I don't know,' I said, looking away.

'Don't lie to me, Jen. I could tell by the way you looked at me, the way your body responded to me in my bed that you weren't faking it. Have you forgotten about that?'

His arm was curled round the back of the sofa and the proximity to the promised delights of his body was tantalising. How could I possibly forget what it was like to share his bed. It was like nothing I'd ever experienced before. If I was just able to put enough distance between me and Alex then maybe I'd have the smallest chance of forgetting I'd ever met him, but every time I saw him it just rendered my defences even weaker.

Thank God we were in Angie and Tom's living room or else I'm sure we would have dispensed with the talk and just fallen into each other's arms. The electricity between us was hard to ignore, but I'd always known instinctively that I wanted more than Alex was ever able to offer me. Hadn't he told me as much?

'You and me, we could have such a great time together. Let's go out. As a proper couple. I promise you it doesn't have to involve any more extreme sports. Not if you don't want it to, that is. Although, I quite fancy bungee jumping. What do you reckon?'

'Absolutely no way. Never in a month of Sundays. I think my adventurous gene has been fully satiated now, thank you.'

He laughed, a mix of fondness and frustration clouding his eyes. 'Okay, I get that, but there's plenty of other stuff you and I could do together.'

He was playing with my head, teasing me, tempting with a future that I hadn't even allowed myself to consider.

'Alex, you and I are different people. I like you, you know that, and I really enjoy your company, but we want different things from life.'

'Ha, that's exactly what I mean.' He picked up my hand, giving it a squeeze, an imploring look on his face. 'You're overthinking things. How can you possibly know what I want from life? You've never asked me. I want to see you. Isn't that enough? To have you as part of my life. Not just meeting up at weddings, christenings and funerals.'

I shrugged a laugh. 'We have spoken about it! You've told me you don't do serious relationships. Three months and you're moving on. That time I saw you, when you told me about Clare, you were warning me off. Telling me I shouldn't allow myself to be hurt in the same way as she was. I get it, Alex. I'm fine with that. Honest, I am.'

'You're clearly not, Jen, and that's what this is all about, isn't it? I don't think you've been hearing me properly. I wasn't warning you off, quite the opposite. What I was trying to explain to you, and clearly I made a very bad job of it, was that most of my relationships haven't moved beyond the three-month mark, but that's not a conscious decision on my part. I don't keep a calendar, marking the days off until a certain date and then walking away. It happens organically, a natural parting, more often than not a mutual thing between two people.'

I raised my eyebrows at him.

'Well, not always mutually, but sometimes,' he added, with a killer smile. 'That didn't happen between us, Jen. The more I saw of you the more I wanted to see you. But every time we seem to get close you take a few steps backwards. I'm too old to be playing games, second guessing what you may or may not be feeling. I want you in my life, Jen. Isn't that enough?'

'Oh, I don't know,' I sighed, my gaze travelling round the room, anxious to escape from the intensity of his scrutiny. I hadn't expected this conversation today.

Was he right though? From the moment I'd met him I'd had a preconceived idea about the sort of person he was, based mainly on what Angie had told me, but partly on some assumptions I'd made myself. It had been difficult not to. In his expensive Italian designer suit, shiny shoes and highly groomed appearance, he cut quite the picture of the type of man your mother warned you to avoid: smooth, polished and sophisticated, a million miles away from the guys I usually met.

I quickly learnt he was an ex-trader who was now the owner of an art gallery. He drove a smart sports car and seemed to live the high life enjoying expensive wines and restaurants. According to Angie, he was a commitment-phobe who'd left a string of glamorous girlfriends in his wake. All in all it painted a pretty convincing picture to me of someone who was undoubtedly intriguing, but probably best avoided if I wanted to keep my heart intact. If anything, in the time I'd got to know Alex better my opinion of him hadn't really changed at all.

'It wouldn't work out between us, that's all.'

'Tell me why not?'

'Why not?' I sighed, much louder than I'd intended and a couple of people turned to look at me so I made an elaborate show of turning the sigh into a not very convincing yawn. 'Well, because I'd fall in love with you and then you'd break my heart and run off with some lovely lithe gorgeous creature leaving me heartbroken.' I waved my arm with a flourish hoping he'd pick up on the lightness of my tone, but as I heard the words hanging in the air, I realised I'd probably just nailed my concerns right there.

'Jen, if you're ever going to love someone again you're going to have to open your heart to that sort of risk. That's what being in love is all about. You do make yourself vulnerable. But don't you think some risks are worth taking?'

I shrugged. Trouble was, I suspected Alex offered a much higher risk value than most other men.

'It might surprise you to know that since I met you I've not been on any other dates. Not one. And the only reason for that is because I haven't wanted to. The only woman I've been interested in seeing is you.'

'Oh,' I said, nursing the stem of my champagne flute. 'Really?'
'Really.'

'Hmm. What about the owner of those silver teardrop earrings then? Have you not seen her again either?'

No sooner had I said the words than I regretted them. Alex didn't owe me any explanations, but those damn earrings had haunted me from the day I'd spotted them, taunting me with all their silver shininess.

'Okay, that was unfortunate and I'm sorry you had to see those. I can imagine how they must have made you feel.'

It was heartening to know that Alex knew exactly what I was talking about.

'I'm not going to make any excuses. It was someone I met, someone I spent the night with, but that was long before I'd even met you. It was just a one-off. I didn't see her again, well only to return the earrings. But I'm telling the truth when I say there hasn't been anyone else since I met you. I've been hanging on hoping that you might change your mind, see the error of your ways, and give me a bloody chance.' He gave a wry smile. 'To be honest, I haven't wanted to see anyone else.'

I shrugged, grateful that the mystery of the earrings had been resolved but hating myself for having needed to ask. Although what Alex was telling me made my heart twist. It must have taken a lot for him to open up like that.'

'I know you've been hurt in the past, Jen, but then so have a lot of other people. Sometimes you have to pick yourself up again and decide what it is you actually want from life. And finding love always involves an element of risk. I know I wouldn't want to spend the rest of my life avoiding getting close to someone just in case they hurt me at some unforeseen date in the future.' Now it was Alex's turn to sigh. 'I can't tell you what's going to happen another three months down the line, or in six months' time or a year. Who knows? It's just as likely that you could run off with your tango instructor and end up breaking my heart but that doesn't stop me from wanting to be with you now.'

'I don't have a tango instructor.'

'Yes, but you might have one in a year's time. And then where will I be?'

I laughed, feeling slightly ridiculous and reprimanded now by the gentle coercing tone to Alex's voice.

'The thing is, Jen, I'm not a clairvoyant. None of us can know what the future has in store for us, but I reckon some things are worth taking a chance on and I would hope that you might think that we, you and me, are worth that chance.'

I pondered that thought for a moment. The heat of the sun on my back was much more insistent now and, aided by the restorative effects of the pink champagne, I'd felt the muscles in my back and neck relax into the contours of the sofa. I'd wanted to change my life and I was beginning to do that in certain areas. Maybe it was time to take a chance too in my personal life.

'Ah,' I stuck my finger in the air, hit by a moment of blinding realisation, 'but you see, I knew there was a good reason for me not to trust you.'

He screwed up his face at me, the unasked question all too evident in his features.

'You told me when we first met that you had special psychic abilities. Don't you remember? You looked at my palm and told me you could see my whole future laid out in front of me. Are you now saying that was all an elaborate charade just to get me into bed,' I said in mock outrage.

Alex dropped my hand and tipped his head back, his gaze landing on the ceiling. He inched himself back along the sofa putting some distance between us.

'I do remember that! And the note I wrote to you. And, from

memory, everything I put in that letter I would still stand by today. But sometimes you have to give fate a helping hand and if you're not prepared to do that, Jen, then there isn't really much more I can say.' Frustration tempered his words. 'I've tried, Jen, really I have, but if you don't want this, us, then however sad that makes me, I have to respect your decision.'

He stood up and I felt a disproportionate amount of disappointment swelling in my body.

What was he doing? Where was he going? I wanted to grab him by the arm and pull him down next to me again. This conversation was only now beginning to get interesting.

'Now, if you'll excuse me, I'm going to find that gorgeous goddaughter of mine again for one of her lovely cuddles.'

23

The calls and texts from Alex stopped in the weeks following the christening and while I'd mentally prepared myself for that eventuality, I was surprised by the depth of the regret and disappointment I felt at not seeing his name light up on my phone, at him not being there – a small shining light in my life, offering a beacon of hope, anticipation and hugely enjoyable sex.

I was still busy temping, making plans for the future, helping Gramps with some important and time consuming shopping, redecorating my flat, but in amongst all the busyness there was still a sense of loss for something that I hadn't even realised I'd had.

I thought about Alex all the time, wondering if I hadn't been a complete and utter fool by not heeding his words and giving our fledgling relationship a chance. I suspected he wouldn't be mooning around, wasting any time on wondering what I was doing or who I was doing it with. He wasn't that type. He'd laid down a pretty good campaign, had given it his all, but had known when to walk away when he thought there wasn't a hope.

'Jen, darling, are you here? Or are you off with the fairies?

This is my first night out since the baby was born but I'm wondering if I might have been better off staying home with Liberty. She certainly would have been more entertaining company.'

'Oh God, I'm sorry,' I said, snapping back into the moment, realising I'd been wrapped up in my own thoughts for the last half an hour.

'Look I'll tell you what, this place is a bit of a dump.' We'd found ourselves in a pub which was tired and past its best, full of mainly young loved-up couples eating their steak and chips, and felt slightly out of place. 'Let's go somewhere else, somewhere a bit more happening, a bit more hip, a bit more us.'

I giggled. I wasn't sure we were any of those things, but I was happy to move on.

'I know somewhere,' I said, decisively. 'There's a really nice wine bar down by the river.' I hadn't been there since the day of the wedding, but now I had a burning, over-riding desire to go there again. I wasn't sure why. It wasn't as if Alex would be there. Or that silly note would still be waiting for me behind the bar. But I just knew I needed to go there, now, tonight, dragging Angie along with me, screaming and kicking, if necessary.

'Oh, this is much better,' said Angie, when we arrived. She led the way through the doors and I followed her, with still a tiny part of me expecting to see Alex sitting at a table waiting for me.

'Ah, Miss Faraday,' he would say, James Bond like. 'I've been expecting you. Come and sit down beside me. I have something for you.'

My head even did a quick scan around all the nooks and crannies of the wine bar just to double-check if he was there or not and there was a ridiculous sense of disappointment when I realised he wasn't. What could I possibly have been expecting?

'I'll go and order, Ange.'

'Don't worry, they'll be over in a minute.'

'No, it's okay,' I said with a smile, completely ignoring Angie's puzzled expression. I wandered over to the bar and ordered two glasses of Prosecco from the young good-looking barman, peering over his shoulder at the extensive well-stocked bar.

'There you go. That's fifteen pounds, please.'

He handed over the payment terminal and I tapped it with my card, deciding, in that moment, if I didn't do it now then I never would.

'I know this might seem a strange thing to ask, but I wondered if there was a letter for me behind the bar. My name's Jen Faraday.'

He looked at me blankly. 'What sort of letter? From the manager, you mean?'

'No, nothing like that. It was a letter from a friend of mine, a customer. We were here this time last year and we had this funny little agreement, like a bet, and he left a letter for me, behind the bar, but with strict instructions that I couldn't open it until about now. So, I'm here to collect it.'

Half a smile lifted one corner of his mouth.

'Right, can't say I've seen anything like that. Let me go and have a look.'

He went off to the main till station and I watched him all the way. He looked underneath the counter, pulled out a small black cash box and opened it up, before quickly closing it again and returning it to its spot. He pulled out an A4 reservations book and flicked through its pages. He spoke to another bartender, who shrugged a response and shook his head, and then he wandered back in my direction.

'Sorry no. I've had a good look but can't find anything. It's quite a long time ago now and most of us wouldn't have been here then. Was it very important?'

'No, not really, it was just a fun thing,' but as I heard my words trail away, I realised, suddenly, just how important it had been to me to find that letter and read what was inside. I masked my disappointment with a smile. 'Thanks for looking though.'

I should have just asked Alex what he'd written in that damned note or we could have come back together to find it and laughed over what he'd written and been reminded of how we'd met and the lovely day we'd shared together at Angie and Tom's wedding. Oh shit! I hurried back to Angie who was sitting waiting impatiently.

'I've just had an awful thought. Did I miss your wedding anniversary?'

'Yep,' she said gleefully, raising her glass to me.

'Oh God, I am so sorry! What kind of friend am I?'

'A forgetful one? Nah, don't worry. So much has happened in this last year I have trouble keeping up with it all myself. We had an Indian takeaway and a bottle of champagne to celebrate. It was lovely actually.'

'Oh, you should have said something. I would have been more than happy to babysit.'

She laughed, looking radiantly happy.

'We thought about it, but we decided we'd both actually prefer to stay in with Liberty. But give us another couple of months and you know we're going to be making full use of all the offers of babysitting we've had from our friends. You know, Jen, I don't know what I spent all that time worrying about. Everything seems to have fallen into place since Liberty arrived. We're really happy, she's such a little sweetheart and Tom is simply besotted with her.' A dreamy expression spread over her features, before her familiar throaty laugh resonated around the wine bar. 'Oh God, I've become one of those awfully smug mums who can bore for England on the marvellousness of her own baby.'

'No you're not. Besides, as godmother, I would have to agree with you that she is simply the best, most beautiful baby there has ever been. And that's not an opinion. That's fact. I'm just so happy for you all.'

'Excuse me.' We were interrupted by the bartender I'd spoken to earlier. 'You're in luck. It was in the main office at the back,' he said, handing over the envelope as if it was a Golden Ticket giving me a pass to all sorts of wonderful delights.

'Ooh, what's that?' said Angie, leaning across the table trying to sneak a look.

'Oh, it's just a letter,' I said, glibly, trying to make out it was a normal everyday occurrence type of thing. 'From Alex.'

'From Alex?' she repeated, her eyes growing wide as she snatched the envelope from my hands. 'Why is Alex sending you a letter? And here of all places? What's going on, Jen?' she asked.

'Oh, it's nothing. Just a silly little thing we had going when we met. We came here the night of your wedding. Did I tell you?'

She shook her head, looking at me amazed, as though I'd committed a cardinal sin in not mentioning it.

'It must have slipped my mind,' I explained. 'He wrote me this note and left it behind the bar. Apparently he's predicted my whole future in here. It was just a bit of a giggle really, but he told me I couldn't open it until at least one year after we met. I'd forgotten all about it until we got here.'

I ignored the doubtful look she was giving me and instead faffed around with the buckle on my handbag before putting the letter away in the side zipped pocket.

'Oh, come on, aren't you going to read it then? You've got me intrigued now. I'm dying to know what's inside there.'

So was I, but I'd waited a year; a few more hours wouldn't hurt. I felt fearful now, though of what I wasn't sure. Half of me wanted to rip the paper apart and read the note and the other half of me wanted to preserve it for when I got back to the sanctuary of my own place. When I was all alone. The only trouble was, Angie was looking at me expectantly, in between checking her watch for the time.

'Look, I'm going to have to get back for Liberty soon. Are you going to read that thing or not? I'll read it for you if you like.'

'No! What if he's said something rude, something he wanted to keep private.'

'Ooh, the sly old dog. What do you mean, like an erotic ode listing all the filthy things he wants to do to you? Well, if that's the case, then you definitely have to open it now.'

I fumbled with my bag again and pulled out the envelope, wondering if I was being disloyal even talking to Angie about it. I stroked the envelope, my finger tracing around the outline of the big, expansive handwriting.

'You're not to breathe a word of this. Not even to Tom. Do you promise me? I don't want Alex thinking I've been talking about him behind his back and he probably won't want people knowing about something he did over a year ago.'

'I promise. Girl guide's honour,' she said, giving me a three-fingered salute. 'Just read the bloody thing, would you.'

I carefully prised open the letter and pulled out the paper, unfolding it in front of me.

'Blimey,' said Angie, noticing the writing on either side of the paper, 'that's not a note, that's a bloody novel. What can he possibly be saying? Read it before it kills me.'

I took a deep breath and started reading.

Saturday 19th April

Dear Jen,

Today I met the woman I'm going to marry. You think that's mad? Well, just think how I feel! You can probably imagine this was a pretty momentous occasion for me and I hope it will come to mean the same to you one day, as you, Jen, are the woman I've fallen so unexpectedly, so suddenly, in love with.

Now, I suspect if I told you this outright, at this moment, as we sit sharing a rather nice of bottle of wine together, after only knowing each other for a matter of hours, that my disclosure would send you running in the opposite direction. You would quite rightly think me a madman or a drunkard at the very least and while it's true that I have had far too much to drink today, I know that this thunderbolt that has struck me hard on the head and in the heart has nothing to do with the amount of alcohol I've consumed.

Funny really, I've heard other people talk about meeting that special someone, maybe even just picking them out across a crowded room, and knowing, almost instantly, that that person is the one; the one they are going to spend the rest of their lives with. I never really believed those things could happen so to find that it's actually happening to me, here and now, is mind blowing to say the least.

I'm tempted to come clean, to tell you now in this nicely mellow mood we've created together, exactly how I feel, but I know it would be foolish. There's no doubting the chemistry, the simmering tension between us, but, to me, it's much much more than that. I'm surprised you can't tell the effect you've had on me by the way I can't keep my eyes off you and the way a stupid smile has fixed itself to my lips. I'm not arrogant enough to believe that you could be experiencing the same strength of feeling as me, but I really hope you like me. I think you do.

No, I have to bide my time and hope to goodness that you like me enough to want to see me again, that we can start dating and get to know each other better. Do things the proper, accepted way, although if it was up to me I would take you home with me tonight and never let you go so we could start the rest of our lives together right now! I want to know every single thing there is to know about you, Jen, all the depths and secrets that are hidden behind those beautiful green eyes of yours.

So you see, Jen, your future is all too clear to me. I don't need to look at your hand to see what's in store for you because it's already written in the stars, but much more importantly it's etched into my heart too. Your future is with me. Forever. Together.

Obviously I can see there will need to be some areas of negotiation. I always imagined having four children; two girls and two boys, but I must admit you looked slightly shocked at that suggestion. Still, these are mere incidentals, we can thrash out the detail at a later date ;)

I really hope you get to read this letter one day and that my predictions come true. If I was laying money on it, then I would say it's a dead cert, but obviously I realise it's not only me involved in the decision making process and there is the possibility that you might actually hate me and choose never to see me again. If that's the case then obviously I would have to accept your decision, but at the risk of sounding scarily stalkerish, I really hope and believe that won't be the case.

But if it is, then this letter will be redundant, and you'll no doubt forget you ever met me. One thing is for sure though, Jen, I will never forget you. And I hope I will never have need to because if things go the way they're destined to then you'll be at my side for the rest of our lives.

So, Jennifer Faraday, will you please marry me?
Lots of love, today, tomorrow and always,
Alex xxx

I took another big breath but this time neatly folded the piece of paper in half, returning it to its envelope.

'Well,' said Angie, clearly impatient now. 'What did it say? You've gone all blotchy up your neck.'

'No, I'm fine,' I said, fanning myself with the envelope. I knew I'd gone all blotchy from the tingling on my skin and the hot fire burning in my veins. My head was doing a merry dance too. 'I'm really sorry, darling, but I can't tell you what it says. Not until I've spoken to Alex and then once I have, I promise, I'll tell you everything about it.'

24

'Hello, Jen, it's Polly here.'

'Hi Polly!' After a rocky start, my relationship with Ms Powers had moved on to a new level of understanding. In her own sweet way, I think she almost quite liked me now.

'Listen, I've had a brilliant new assignment come in this morning and immediately I thought of you. Would you be interested?'

'Oh God!' I groaned, the words slipping out before I had a chance to stop them. A huge ball of dread lodged in the centre of my chest. I hardly dared ask. 'What is it?'

'It's a six-week assignment working for an electrical contractors. They want someone to go in to take an inventory of items that have come back into stock from different outlets around the country. Then the information would need to be transferred onto their internal database system. It sounds very straightforward.'

Straightforward, but incredibly boring.

'Thanks for thinking of me, Polly,' I said with a huge sense of freedom and relief, 'but to be honest with you I couldn't really commit to a job for that length of time right now.'

It was true. In the last couple of weeks life had become incredibly hectic. One afternoon a week I was running a kitchen garden course at the local arts centre. I was writing a monthly column for the community magazine, planning a series of one-day workshops for later on in the year, and my Insta posts were gaining traction and my followers increasing all the time.

'Are you sure? I could probably negotiate an increase in the hourly rate if that might help your decision.'

I smiled into the telephone. There wasn't enough money in this world to convince me to lose six weeks of my life to counting electrical components. Ball bearings had been bad enough.

'Absolutely certain. In fact, it's probably best if you take my details down for the moment. I can't see that I'm going to be able to take on any more assignments in the near future.'

'Okay, well thanks for letting me know,' said the lovely Polly. 'If things change, then do get in touch and I can put you back up on our system.'

Putting down the phone, I felt a small swell of affection for Polly and her team. She'd offered me a lifeline when I'd needed one and I'd always be grateful to her for that. If things ever got really bad and I was desperate to earn a bit of money then I knew Polly would do her utmost to help me out. While none of the temporary work I'd undertaken had offered me the stimulating challenge I'd been searching for, it had shown me what it was like to be working out in the big wide world. I wasn't sure I liked it much. If anything it had only confirmed to me that working for myself, pursuing my own creative projects, was where I would be happiest.

I'd just flicked the kettle on when the front doorbell rang.

'Matt! What a lovely surprise! Come in. I was just making a cup of coffee.'

We kept in touch through texts, but it was lovely to see his gorgeous friendly face in the flesh. I led him through into the kitchen and he took a seat at the breakfast bar. He looked all around him, an amused expression on his face as he observed my makeshift office on the kitchen table which was home now to my laptop, my mobile phone, my camera, to-do lists and a selection of half-finished craft projects.

'Well, it certainly looks as though you're busy,' he said, taking the mug I offered him.

'Honestly, I've never been busier. I've got so many different things on the go, but I'm loving every single moment of it. I'm not earning mega bucks but it's enough to pay the rent and to keep me stocked in Prosecco. That's all I need in life, really.' I laughed. 'Of course, I miss Browns tremendously. It takes some getting used to, working on your own with only the radio for company.'

A sorry smile spread across Matt's lips and I felt a pang of sadness for everything I'd left behind. I still couldn't rid myself of the thought that I'd let him down by leaving.

'Honestly, I do, Matt. I miss you and everyone else hugely, but I still think it was the right decision for me to move on.' I took a sip from my coffee. 'How are things at work? Is Emma settling in?'

'Yep, all good. Emma's doing well. She's enthusiastic and keen to learn. I'm trying not to bombard her with too much informa-tion at once though. Of course, what I didn't factor in is that she isn't taking on a clearly defined role. It's only now that you've left that I've realised just how much you took on at work, how much responsibility you had. It was a position that developed and evolved over a number of years and I can't really expect someone else to come in and take on everything that you were doing straight away.'

'No, I suppose that's true. I guess it will take a little time, but it's great that she's so enthusiastic.'

'Yes, well actually that was one of the things I wanted to talk to you about. I wanted to see how you might feel about doing some freelance work for Browns. I'm thinking in particular about the sourcing of products for the kitchen and giftware departments. That was always your speciality, Jen. You seem to have a knack for knowing what's going to be the big sellers for the coming seasons. As you know, I haven't really got any interest in that side of the business and it's something I can't expect Emma to take on just at the moment. If you're interested you'd be doing me a huge favour. You'd probably know better than me, but I'm thinking it would probably be about a day a fortnight?'

I nodded, intrigued about the suggestion.

'That sounds about right.' It was the side of my job that I'd loved the most. Scanning supplier websites and stores, searching out the prettiest and most practical items to fill the shelves. It was a role that would fit in perfectly with all my other projects too and would mean another income stream. I smiled, shaking my head, hardly believing that in such a short space of time everything could have fallen so perfectly into place.

'Thanks for the offer, Matt, I'd love to take you up on that.'

'Good. Well why don't you come into the garden centre one day next week and we can draw up a plan, get the ball rolling. There was just one other thing.'

'Yes,' I asked, intrigued.

'I wanted to float the idea of you coming in and running some weekly workshops, similar to those you do at the arts centre. Also we need to start stocking some of your famous chilli jam. Ever since your put up that story you've become quite the celebrity.'

'Honestly, I could never have anticipated just how popular it would be. In fact, I still haven't replied to all the comments. There were hundreds of them. I've just been so busy, but I really need to get round to doing that soon.'

'Ah!' Matt fell silent for a moment, suddenly looking uncomfortable as he looked from his clasped hands and then across at me. 'Um, you do realise why that post was quite as successful as it was.'

'I think so. I put it down to the fact that it was just a really positive, upbeat post, one of those projects that anyone can have a go at, that you can see through from the very beginning to the end. Growing your own chillies at home, making the jam, decorating the jars and labels. It's a very satisfying thing to do and, of course, the finished product makes such a lovely little gift.'

'Yes, well, I suppose there is that, but um... I'm not quite sure how to tell you this, Jen.'

'What?' It wasn't like Matt to be bashful. 'Matt, please tell me what you're talking about.'

'Did you have a proper look at the photo you posted up, Jen?'

'Yes, of course, it was six pretty jars of chilli jam sitting on my bedroom window. I was quite pleased with that shot actually. I tried them on the kitchen window, in the garden, on the coffee table, but none of them quite worked and then I had a brainwave. Turns out the bedroom window was the perfect place. Who'd have thought?'

'Hmmm, well...' He pulled a face, his mouth contorting awkwardly and I was just beginning to feel a bit uneasy about this whole thing when Matt pulled out his phone and pulled up a screenshot. 'Look, let me show you.'

'Yes, perfect,' I said, feeling the same warm swell of pride I experienced every time I viewed any of my posts. I'd spent ages deciding on the background and was delighted when I found the pretty ivy design. It looked just as I'd intended it to; pretty, fresh and clean.

'Over here on the side, Jen,' he said, completely ignoring my pretty design and pointing to the photo of the jars of chilli jam. I looked at them, bemused. It took a moment, but then the penny dropped.

'You are kidding me, no!' I threw his phone back at him and jumped out of my seat, standing with my back against the cooker, putting as much distance as I possibly could between me and the phone. 'No, oh no. Shit, shit, shit. No.'

I broke into a run there on the spot, swinging my arms across my chest as though I was warming up for a sprint. In fact that was probably the best idea right at that moment. To start running and never to stop. Ever again.

'Oh God, Matt, please tell me it isn't so?'

''Fraid so,' he said, unable to hide the smile twitching at the corners of his mouth.

I sat back down, took a deep breath and prepared to look at the phone again. Maybe it wouldn't look quite so bad second time around. Wrong! If anything, it looked a hundred times worse. There, in the corner of my lovely picture of the chilli jams, was me, reflected in the mirror of my wardrobe, wearing only the skimpiest of underwear, holding my camera up to capture my handiwork. And a whole lot more besides, I realised now.

'Look, it could have been worse,' said Matt.

'How?' I said, close to tears now. 'How could it possibly be any worse?'

'Well, you could have been in the nuddy nude. Just think how embarrassing that would have been.'

'Oh god, I suppose, can you imagine,' I said, with a sigh, wondering how I'd ever be able to set foot outside my home again. 'At least I was in my best matching underwear,' I said, with a reluctant smile.

Matt stood up to give me a hug. 'Look you know what they say, all publicity is good publicity. And it does mean you have a very big fan base now. They're calling you *The Red Hot Chilli Girl*.'

'That's awful, just awful. I'll take the photo down.' I grabbed my phone and my fingers fumbled to delete the offending post with a flourish. 'There!' I said, as if that made everything better.

'Trouble is I think you've probably been saved onto a thousand hard drives by now. Just brazen it out, Jen. Use it as a positive and build on your success. Honestly, it will be absolutely fine. And one day, you'll look back on all this and laugh.'

Ha, ha. I was practising, but no, I couldn't ever see that day coming soon.

Matt walked over to the door to leave. 'Have a think about what I said about doing those workshops. Today's probably not the best day for you to make a decision on that, but I think it would be a great opportunity for you and Browns. You've created quite a demand now, Jen, and there's nothing like striking while the iron's hot.'

As soon as Matt left, I slumped against the door, cradling my head in my arms, before breaking into uncontrollable fits of laughter there on my kitchen floor. What a numpty I'd been. Still, there was nothing I could do about it now. Matt was absolutely right; I needed to make the most of the situation and strike while the iron was hot. I would definitely be taking him up on his offer to run some workshops at the garden centre. Why not? These last few weeks had taught me that I needed to take my chances when I could get them and, along with all the work opportunities coming my way, there was one other big opportunity that I had no intention of overlooking.

I stood and picked up my phone, tapping in the number.

Be bold, be brave, love more!

'Hi Alex,' I said, when he picked up, my heart fluttering at the sound of his voice. 'It's Jen. There's something I wanted to ask you...'

25

We must have looked at every wedding venue in town, from the cute and quaint to the chic and sophisticated. What we decided on very early on was that we wanted something fairly intimate, for about forty guests, and in the end, after looking much further afield, we plumped for the local Royal British Legion Club, just down the road, familiar and cosy.

The room was transformed from a fairly standard function hall into a magical romantic oasis by the addition of cream silk roof drapes, a fairy light canopy, roses and peonies along the length of the tables and twinkling topiary trees. Even if I said so myself, I'd done a pretty amazing job.

'Have I told you, you look absolutely gorgeous today,' said Gramps, coming up to me for a hug as I took a moment to look around and appreciate that, despite all my worries, the sleepless nights and the last minute panics over the table decorations, the day had been a roaring success. It was the first time I'd been able to properly relax all day, but now that the formalities were over, people had their plates piled high from the amazing buffet provided by a catering friend and the wine and beer were flowing, I was determined to enjoy every single last moment of this happy occasion.

'Do you really think so?' I said, giving him a twirl. I'd tried on every dress within a twenty-mile radius of home and discarded each of them before deciding on a two-piece cream flared trouser suit. I hoped it gave off just the right impression. I hadn't wanted anything too frilly, flouncy or frou frou. I was going for feminine and understated, and judging by the complimentary comments I'd already received I think I'd achieved it.

'Beautiful! And what you've done here, it's just simply amazing. Marcia couldn't believe her eyes when she saw it. You really are such a talented and lovely girl. I'm so lucky to have you as my granddaughter, you mean the world to me, you know that. And Marcia too.'

'Aw, Gramps, you're looking pretty dapper yourself. I don't think I've ever seen you looking so smart. And I'm the lucky one having you as my Gramps.'

'Well, you know,' he said, his voice giving a little wobble, 'I didn't want to let anyone down today.'

'What? Are you kidding me? You could never do that, Gramps.' I gazed up into his moistened eyes and then straightened up the flower in his buttonhole. 'Don't you dare go all soppy on me. I'm just about holding it together as it is.'

He dabbed his eyes with a handkerchief before kissing me on the forehead.

'Anyway, where is that young man of yours hiding? I've not had a chance to speak to him properly yet.'

'I'll go and get him,' I said. I spotted Alex over the other side of the room and gestured for him to come and join us. When I'd seen him for the first time that morning, dressed in a soft grey three-piece suit, my heart had filled and I'd known instinctively that I was doing absolutely the right thing. To be honest, I couldn't understand why I'd fought my feelings for so long. Alex had been absolutely right. Sometimes you just had to take that first step and see where it took you.

He was definitely the best looking man in the building, apart from Gramps of course, and to see the pair of them together meant the world to me. Even Harvey, another of my favourite men, was here too, sat in the corner, with some of Gramps' friends from the bowls club, taking the opportunity to hoover up any crumbs of food that fell to the floor.

'Mr Faraday,' said Alex now, holding out his hand to Gramps and shaking it vigorously. 'Many congratulations to you and your new wife. It's been a marvellous day.'

'Thank you, son,' said Gramps, 'and that's mainly down to my clever granddaughter here. She's organised it all, under Marcia's instructions, of course. And please, it's Harry. I don't want any of that Mr Faraday nonsense.'

'Harry it is then,' said Alex, smiling. 'I've just been chatting to Marcia actually. She's been telling me all about the dance you've been practising. I can't wait to see that.'

'Oh dear. I was hoping Marcia might have forgotten about that now she's had a couple of glasses of sherry, but it doesn't sound like it. I just hope I can remember what I should be doing or else I will be in trouble.'

'You'll be brilliant, Gramps. Just let the music and Marcia guide you round the floor. You know everyone will be rooting for you anyway.'

'Yes, I've been overwhelmed with everyone turning up today, and all the good wishes we've received. Right, well, I suppose I ought to go and find my good lady wife then,' he smiled to himself, as though he couldn't actually believe he could now rightly use those words again. Gramps wasn't the type of man to be alone. He needed a good woman in his life and I was thankful that Marcia had filled that gap. Before we'd left for the registry office this morning, he and I had taken a moment together to remember Nan and Mum, and had raised a glass of champagne in their memory.

'Thanks so much for coming today, Alex. It's lovely to see Jen with a twinkle in her eye these days.'

'Gramps,' I said, groaning, giving him a surreptitious dig in the ribs.

Alex laughed. 'It's my absolute pleasure and thank you for inviting me. I've had a wonderful time.' When Gramps had wandered off to find Marcia, Alex took me by the hand. 'He's a great guy, your granddad, and they make a lovely couple, don't they? There's something about love in later years that warms the heart, don't you think? Well, love at any age, come to that.'

'Oh definitely. I'm just pleased they're so happy and have one another to look out for each other.'

'Yep, isn't that what everyone's looking for? That special person to be with, who will always be at your side, someone to support, love and nourish you, whatever stage in life you're at.'

He grabbed hold of my hand and squeezed my fingers tight and looking into his eyes I sensed there was a whole lot of meaning in that squeeze.

'Yes, I guess so,' I said with a smile. I felt as though I'd climbed a mountain, traversed a desert and swum the widest lake in the world these last few weeks. After my embarrassment of being exposed to the local community as a tomato and then having my near naked body spread around the internet, life had settled down into some kind of normality in recent weeks. I'd had so many offers of work it was untrue. Some very exciting and some highly dubious, but I was determined to consider each of them on their own individual merits.

Now I was ready to take that next step on my journey to

opening up my heart and finding that special person to share the rest of my life with. I had a pretty good idea I wouldn't need to go very far to find him now.

'You know it really means a lot to me that you asked me to be your plus one today. I was surprised, but, as you can see, absolutely delighted to accept.'

We stood in silence for a moment watching as the four-piece band took up their positions and started warming up. They quickly started on their set, playing some oldie recognisable tunes and the energy in the room moved up a notch.

'You know, I went back to collect your note. The one you left in the wine bar for me.'

'You did? Oh...' He narrowed his eyes at me, a half smile forming at his lips. 'I thought you'd probably forgotten all about that by now. Well,' he shrugged. 'I always intended for you to read it, Jen.'

'Yes,' I gulped, swallowing the emotion that was bubbling inside me. 'I was intrigued to know what was in there. I just happened to be in the wine bar and curiosity got the better of me.'

'O-kay,' he said, giving me a sideways glance that sent a flutter of excitement racing around my body. 'So what did you think when you read it? Did you think I was a madman?'

'No. Well not really,' I laughed. 'I know you only meant it as a bit of fun.'

'No, that's the thing, Jen, it wasn't.' His voice was impassioned, stirring a response from deep down within my tummy. 'It wasn't meant to be a bit of fun at all. I was deadly serious.' His hand touched my cheek, his gaze roaming my face. 'I meant every word in that letter. I knew from the first moment I saw you that you were the woman for me.'

He paused long enough for my pulse to pick up a pace as his

eyes, full of sincerity, locked onto mine. 'Everything written in that note came from the heart and there was no one more surprised than me by the depth of feeling I instantly had for you. Although we'd only just met it was like I'd known you for ever. It's never happened to me before and I wouldn't expect it to happen to me again. The feelings I felt for you that day haven't changed over all these months, Jen. Honestly. And that's why I haven't wanted to date anyone else in the meantime. That's why I'm still here. Some things are worth waiting for.'

'Really?' My voice came out in a whisper.

'Yes. I know you weren't feeling it in the same way so I was just biding my time, waiting for you to come to your senses.' His mouth curled up in a smile and he stroked my cheek with his thumb. 'Took a bit longer than I expected, mind you. I was beginning to wonder if you were going to prove completely immune to my charms.'

'Oh Alex, I didn't know what to think. You were unlike anyone I'd ever met before, you were certainly not the type of person I usually go for and I suppose, after what Angie told me, I was just scared I would end up getting hurt. And I couldn't face that, but now I realise how I feel about you and I'm prepared to take that risk. I really want us to try and make a go of it.'

'That's all I've ever wanted,' said Alex. 'Me and you, Jen, it's going to be absolutely great.' He kissed me long and hard to a rousing cheer from the bowls club crowd, before we pulled apart, laughing. 'Hey, look at Gramps, he's waltzing around that floor like he's Anton du Beke.'

As other people stood up to join the bride and groom in the dancing, Alex turned to me. 'So is it official, can I call you my girlfriend/partner/love-of-my life/future wife?' he asked.

'All four, preferably.'

'Good because I want you to know, Jen, that I love you with all my heart.'

His words sent a squidgy, oozing sensation trickling through my veins. I didn't need to think about it. I'd been fighting my feelings for far too long, but not for a single moment longer.

'I love you too, Alex.'

'Brilliant, and about bloody time,' he said, those twinkling eyes of his gently chastising me. He kissed me on the lips, sending delicious ripples of delight to every part of my body, and I swayed into his embrace. 'In that case, would you please give me the honour of this dance?' he asked, holding out his hand to me.

'I'd be absolutely delighted,' I said with a wide smile as my future husband led me out onto the dance floor.

ACKNOWLEDGEMENTS

Thank you for reading my book! I really hoped you enjoyed Jen and Alex's story.

The idea for this novel first came about many years ago after watching a documentary about a registrar's office. It was a fascinating and emotional insight into people's lives as they visited the office to register their births, deaths and marriages. One particular item, about a couple getting married on a whim and dragging a couple of strangers off the street to witness the event, stayed with me.

Initially I wrote a short story based on that idea, naming it *Take a Chance*, which was published in *Best* magazine in 2014, but the characters of the witnesses, renamed to Jen and Alex, wouldn't go away. I wondered what their story might be if they were to meet up again and that's how this novel came into being. It was first published as an ebook in 2016.

I'm hugely grateful to my publishers, Boldwood Books, for giving this story an update, a lovely new cover and making it available in all formats, including audio and paperback, to a whole new audience.

A big thank you and much love, as always, to my family and friends, and finally, a huge thanks to you, my valued readers, for your continued support.

ABOUT THE AUTHOR

Jill Steeples is the author of many successful women's fiction titles – most recently the Dog and Duck series - all set in the close communities of picturesque English villages. She lives in Bedfordshire.

Sign up to Jill Steeples' mailing list here for news, competitions and updates on future books.

Visit Jill's website: www.jillsteeples.co.uk

Follow Jill on social media:

facebook.com/jillsteepleswriter

x.com/jillesteeples

instagram.com/jill.steeples

ALSO BY JILL STEEPLES

When We Meet Again

Maybe This Christmas?

It's Now or Never

Primrose Woods Series

Starting Over at Primrose Woods

Snowflakes Over Primrose Woods

Dreams Come True at Primrose Hall

Starry Skies Over Primrose Hall

Sunny Sundays at Primrose Hall

Dog & Duck Series

Winter at the Dog & Duck

Summer at the Dog & Duck

Wedding Bells at the Dog & Duck

Happily-Ever-After at the Dog & Duck

LOVE NOTES

LOVE IN EVERY CHAPTER

WHERE ALL YOUR ROMANCE
DREAMS COME TRUE!

THE HOME OF BESTSELLING
ROMANCE AND WOMEN'S
FICTION

 WARNING:
MAY CONTAIN SPICE

SIGN UP TO OUR
NEWSLETTER

https://bit.ly/Lovenotesnews

Boldwood

Printed in Great Britain
by Amazon

44573592R00126